The Garden Party

Millie Curtis

Avid Readers Publishing Group
Lakewood, California

The Garden Party

Avid Readers Publishing Group

http://www.avidreaderspg.com

ISBN-13: 978-1-61286-373-3

Acknowledgements

My thanks to Curtis Nishimoto, Elizabeth Blye, and Amy Nishimoto for their various skills in getting this story ready for publishing. Also, to Eric for making an exception.

Chapter 1

Catherine Burke was having coffee on the side porch with her husband, Patrick. As he sat reading, her mind drifted to how her life had changed over the past five years. Once the town milliner, destined to be a spinster by the gossip of the community, she was now the wife of a respected physician and the mother of three young children.

The country had survived the Great War, women over thirty had gained the right to vote, and the future was promising, and the fact that she was turning thirty was pushed to the back of her mind.

She smiled to herself as she remembered how Patrick had come into her life one morning requesting repair of his mother's hat. He was from Washington, and they were in town for a notable wedding.

The early morning Virginia sun warmed the room where Patrick was engrossed in reading the weekly edition of *The Clarke Courier.* Catherine was daydreaming as she looked out the window at the sprawling lawn of their Victorian home on South Church Street, one of the fine streets in the small town of Berryville. The English boxwoods made a pretty hedge. A small goldfish pond sparkled in the sunlight, and the flower gardens would soon be in bloom.

"Patrick, we've been invited to a garden party."

He turned the page of the paper without looking up.

"The invitation is from Elizabeth and Andrew Caldwell. I want to go."

They sat in silence until Patrick looked over at her and folded the paper. "I'm sorry. Now what is this about a garden party?"

With a slight edge to her tone, she said, "Apparently you haven't been listening to me."

"I caught some of it." He looked over at her and smiled. Catherine could never resist his smile. "I was captured by one of Lavinia's prattles about Dr. and Mrs. Hawthorne going to visit relatives in Pennsylvania. The local news is full of noteworthy items."

"Hah," she replied. "I know better than that. You can't stand Lavinia Talley. As the editor's wife she's right where she wants to be, right on top of the social scene and everything in between."

"I'm glad she's a patient of Thad's and not mine." He finished his coffee, rose and stretched his slim body. "I need to head to the office. With Thaddeus away, the place is jumping."

Catherine stood up, walked over to him, reached out, and twisted a lock of his dark-brown hair with her fingers. "You need a haircut," she said.

He leaned down and kissed her smooth cheek. "I'm too busy." His clear blue eyes were alive. "Why don't you walk on down into town at noon, and we'll go for lunch. Just the two of us and we'll forget the outside world. We used to be able to do that. Remember?"

Catherine smiled and gave a soft sigh. "Our lives have changed a lot in these five years, haven't they? If Mattie can watch the little ones, I'll put on a pretty dress, my fancy hat, and prance on down to meet you. Who knows? Maybe I'll make next week's *Courier*: *Mrs. Catherine Burke, the former milliner, joined her husband for lunch at the popular Battletown Inn last Wednesday.*"

Patrick smiled. "You forgot to say what we ate, but you might get a job as a reporter. You could give Lavinia a run for the money."

Catherine laughed. "Run? Lavinia? I don't think she could run for anything except the *Queen of Gossip*."

"Probably right," he said.

Catherine fingered the material in the new three-piece suit he wore. "You look smart in that outfit."

"Eustace decks me out right fine." In a playful mood, he reached out and snared her waist. "And, Mrs. Burke, you look right fine in that lacy robe. I'd rather stay right here. We can sneak up the back stairs before the little ones wake up."

"The little ones who put a few extra pounds on me," she answered.

Patrick looked directly into her green eyes. "You're just as attractive as that first day I saw you sweeping the sidewalk in front of your shop."

She shook her head and gave a big sigh. "It seems so long ago. Weren't we the lucky ones?"

Then she threw her arms around his neck and kissed him soundly.

He gave her a tight squeeze before he released her. "You are a temptress, but duty calls." Patrick turned and left the room, took his straw boater hat from the side table in the foyer, and opened the front door to the wide porch. "I'll see you at noon," he called back to her.

Catherine felt an inner glow as she watched her husband jauntily trip down the sidewalk for his day of treating patients. Rustling noises from upstairs alerted her that the children were awake, so she hurried up the back stairs to her room to change from her robe. Once the three were up the day would no longer belong to her.

As she changed into a day dress, her mind went back to the thought of going to Elizabeth's party. Patrick didn't appear to be interested. In fact, he hadn't answered. Would he agree or not? She knew he guarded what free time he had, but Andrew and Elizabeth were good friends, and it had been some time since they'd seen them. It seems marriage, children, and earning a living bring changes to life, and not all of them welcome.

On the Burke property, Mattie and Jacob, devoted caretakers, lived in a cottage built for them a short walk from the big house of Patrick and Catherine. It was a quaint spot sheltered by towering oak trees.

Mattie had taken care of Patrick since he was a toddler in Washington. Mattie's mother had been a maid for Patrick's mother, a demanding woman. Mattie's mother had said she had enough to do than to "have a couple young'uns under my feet." Therefore, Mattie, being twelve at that time, became the caretaker for Patrick and his younger brother. As time went on, she looked after Patrick as a mother would look after her son.

That's how it was when Patrick married Catherine. After Patrick and Catherine started living in his house in Georgetown, Mattie looked at Miz' Catherine as an intrusion. It was Mattie's job, not Catherine's, to look after Mistah' Patrick and his house. But the animosity had settled, especially after Mattie had chased a no-good from the property who was attempting to assault Catherine. Mattie was a strong woman.

Now she had the three little Burkes to watch over, and the big house to keep in order. Patrick had hired a younger woman to clean and relieve Mattie of some of the burden, but Mattie remained the boss.

Jacob, Mattie's husband, took care of the grounds. He also had help as he and Mattie were near fifty, and the years do take their toll. The two were a good match as Jacob was quiet and more laid back. If his wife got off to fussing about some minor incident, Jacob let her fuss while he went out and trimmed a bush.

Mattie stretched when she got out of bed and dressed her large frame in a hurry. She found her husband in the little kitchen where he'd brewed a pot of coffee on a two-burner pot-bellied stove and had a bowl of oatmeal ready for her.

"Land sakes, Jacob, why didn't you wake me up? It's near eight o'clock and those little ones are goin' to be up and wantin' to eat."

"Jacob looked at her. You know Miz' Catherine ain't goin' to let them starve. You needed the rest."

"I be fine," she said. "Now I gotta' rush myself over there and get busy."

"Sit down and eat your breakfast," said Jacob. "A few minutes won't make a difference."

Mattie frowned at him, but she took her seat and gobbled down the warm oatmeal after she loaded it with butter and brown sugar.

Jacob poured a mug of coffee for her while she was eating. "I'll clean up the dishes," he said. "You feel all right?"

Mattie didn't look up at him. "I tol 'you, I be fine." She drank the coffee and rose from her chair. "Clean that oatmeal out good so it don't stick to the bowl. I better get on over there and see about my babies."

"Maybe Miz' Catherine should hire a girl to help you with those little ones," suggested Jacob.

Mattie stood with hands on ample hips. "I don't need no help with those sweet babies. Miz' Catherine is right there helpin' me."

Jacob knew by the look on his wife's face that he'd said enough.

Mattie changed her tone, "Is your boy comin' to help you in the yard today? Looks like it's goin' to be a good day to pretty up the place."

"He'll be here soon," answered Jacob. "You gonna be here for lunch?"

"That depends on Miz' Catherine. I don't think she's got any meeting today, but I don't know until I get there. Makes me feel good you doin' the dishes," she said. Perhaps feeling bad for her disgruntled attitude, she smiled at him. "You're a good man, Jacob."

With a concerned look, he watched as Mattie hustled past the boxwood hedge as she went to assume her duties at the big house. She had been mighty tired lately. Jacob shrugged his shoulders. Age? They were both getting on in years.

When she reached the house, Mattie heard the commotion in the kitchen before she opened the door. John Patrick, the four-year-old, ran to meet her.

"Hi Miss Mattie. Mama's trying to make pancakes. Carrie Jo spilled her milk, and Mary Margaret slipped in it."

"Trying is right," said an exasperated Catherine as she rose to her feet from kneeling. She brushed back a strand of her hair with the back of her hand. "I'm cleaning up the milk. Mary isn't hurt, she's just scared, but I had to clean this mess before tending to her." Catherine went to the sink and threw in the soiled dish towel before she washed her hands, yanked a clean dish towel off a wooden rod, and dried them.

Mattie stood with the tearful Mary Margaret in her arms, cooing and patting her back. "I'm sorry I'm late. Jacob let me sleep over the time I usually get up. I'll take over here so you can settle the girls," she said as she handed Mary Margaret to her beleaguered mother.

Catherine hugged her youngest and kissed her cheek. Mary Margaret was calming down with stuttering breaths. "Mama's sorry you fell down."

Mattie took on the role of being in charge. "Johnny, you know how to get the plates, so you help your mama and me," she ordered.

The sun was shining in the south window of the big, high-ceilinged room. Johnny had to stand on a stepstool to open the cupboard to get the plates. The round oak table sat in the middle of the wood-floored kitchen where Catherine was settling the girls into high chairs and pulling them up to the table. "I don't know how you cook those pancakes over that wood stove," Catherine said. "I burned the first three and threw them out to the birds."

The stove, an ornate monstrosity made of iron that had belonged to Patrick's mother, had been popular twenty years earlier, but in the more well-to-do homes, electric stoves were making a statement.

Mattie had tied on her ruffled apron and was busy stirring batter in a round green pottery bowl. "Johnny, you get a couple of graham crackers and give them to your sisters. That'll help 'til I get the cakes goin'."

Catherine was busy washing the girls 'faces and hands. "For this being a beautiful day, I think it's falling apart," she said.

"Why do you say that?" asked Mattie, "It was just a little spilt milk."

"When Mr. Patrick and I were having coffee, before the children were awake, I told him I wanted to attend a garden party. He didn't seem too interested in that idea."

Mattie rolled her eyes with her back turned from Catherine and kept her attention on the pancakes. "I 'spect he thinks you got enough to do with the children and all that other stuff you do."

Catherine was quick with a defensive answer, "I'm expected to help at church, and as Patrick's wife there are certain social functions I must attend. The *Woman's Club of Clarke County* is one of them. I know you don't approve because you think it is only for a select few, but its function is to improve intellectual accomplishment, and do good works for the community."

"You like to use them big words," was Mattie's response.

Catherine ignored Mattie's remark.

John Patrick had given the girls each a cracker and had set the plates on the bare wooden table.

"These little cakes are ready," announced the rescuer of the morning. "Johnny, you bring your plate over so Miss Mattie can give you a couple before your sisters get one."

"John Patrick," said his mother, "you can use the syrup. I'm not going to put anything on the girls' pancakes. I've had enough mess this morning."

Catherine picked up the girls' plates and carried them over to the stove. Under her breath she said to Mattie, "You're going to spoil him."

Mattie just smiled.

John Patrick was busy at the table enjoying his pancakes. "I think Mama said a bad word, Miss Mattie, but she didn't say it out loud."

"Eat your breakfast," said Catherine, and turned so he couldn't see her smile.

To Mattie she said, "I do not recommend having three children in three years."

Mattie went right on turning her cakes. "Miz' Catherine, 'spect you need to count your blessins'," was the reply from the woman who had never borne a child.

An apologetic look came over Catherine's face, and she changed the subject. "I've thought about getting an electric stove. Do you think that would be a good idea?"

"Never cooked over one," replied Mattie. "I don't want some new-fangled thing that I can't work."

"We could learn together. I saw a picture of a pretty porcelain yellow stove in the *McCall's* magazine. It stands on four legs that make it waist high, and has three burners and a side oven. You wouldn't have to fool with wood or bend over to bake in the oven."

"What does Mistah' Patrick say?"

"I haven't asked him yet."

Mattie turned with a skeptical look. "You ain't goin' to make it sound like it's my idea?"

"Of course not," Catherine said.

"Course not," mumbled Mattie.

"Can you watch the children at lunchtime? Patrick asked me to meet him in town for lunch.

I could ask him his opinion. After this morning's fiasco, he might agree that a new stove would be useful." It wouldn't hurt to mention Mattie's name, thought Catherine.

Mattie shook her head, "Uh, um. You do get ideas."

Chapter 2

Catherine sat in the Battletown Inn dining room in a corner, which was as private a spot as one could get in the restaurant. The inn held three dining rooms with wood floors, fireplaces, white tablecloths, and curtained windows. The wood floors announced every patron as the heels of their shoes could be heard clicking and creaking across the floor.

Catherine sat in the middle dining room where a fireplace held a low burning log. Although the May day was pleasant, the night had been cool and the interior of the inn had not caught up to the outdoor temperature.

Harry West, a familiar waiter dressed in a white shirt, black bow tie, and black pants, seated her and brought a pot of hot tea to the table while she waited for Patrick to arrive. The table for two was next to a window, but all that was visible from the window was the stone side of the Hawthorne building that contained the offices of Patrick and Dr. Thaddeus Hawthorne. At least the window allowed some light into the interior room.

Harry West was a dapper man in his thirties. He looked much above the status of a waiter, but he had worked at the inn ever since he arrived in Berryville two years ago. He rented a small apartment above the shoe shop, rarely drove his two-passenger 1911 Maxwell car that he kept in a storage building behind the Main Street buildings, and taught a Sunday school class at the Presbyterian Church. Harry was sociable, although not forthcoming on his past.

Rumors about Harry West flew around town. The gossipers were experts at creating possibilities: Harry had been spurned, Harry liked men instead of women, Harry's family had disowned him, Harry was hiding from the federal authorities.

And, every month Harry sent an envelope to Washington D.C. with an address of only a post office box number. That piqued the curiosity of the clerk in the local post office.

If Harry heard all the rumors, he chose to ignore them, and in all fairness, he was well liked in the community, especially at the inn where he did his best to please the patrons.

Catherine sat thinking about how she was going to pose the question to Patrick about the stove when he arrived with a smile on his clean-shaven face. He looked around at the three empty tables in the room. "Just the two of us? How did you manage that?" he asked as he kissed her rosy cheek before he took his seat at the table.

"I told Harry we wanted a quiet spot because you only have a short time, and it wouldn't do to have any interruptions."

Harry appeared from the door that led to the kitchen. "Dr. Burke?" He was surprised. "How did I miss you coming in?"

"Hello, Harry. You were busy and your back was turned. I believe Mrs. Talley was dissatisfied about something."

If Lavinia had ruffled his feathers, Harry didn't let it show. That was one trait that made him a good waiter. "Mrs. Burke told me you are short on time."

"Until Dr. Hawthorne is back in town. What is the special of the day?"

"Potato soup and a chicken salad sandwich," answered Harry in his excellent diction.

"Perfect," said Patrick. "We'll both have the special."

Harry smiled. "I'll tell the cook to hurry it up," and he went in the direction of the kitchen.

With her voice just above a whisper, Catherine said, "I didn't know Lavinia was here. I hope she didn't see you."

His tone of voice matched hers. "She was too busy dragging Harry over the coals. I assume Mattie is with the children."

"Yes. Jean Marie came over to play. She's old enough to keep an eye on them and help Mattie. I've suggested that we hire another woman to ease the burden because the children are full of energy. It has to be tiring for Mattie, but she won't hear of it. Perhaps you should talk to her. You know how stubborn she can be. She might listen to you before she will listen to me."

"She might," he agreed. "Once Thad gets back, I'll have more time."

Harry brought their lunches and pot of hot tea. Another waiter came into the room leading a young couple unfamiliar to the Burkes.

"I'm sorry," apologized Harry. "We're quite busy today, but I had hoped we could seat everyone in the main dining room giving you more privacy."

"No problem," assured Patrick. "I only have time enough to eat this delicious looking food." Harry nodded and turned to go into the front dining room.

Patrick took a spoon of soup and surprised Catherine with, "What's this about a garden party?"

At least she didn't sputter in her surprise. "You were listening this morning. We haven't seen Andrew and Elizabeth for almost six months. Do you want to go?"

Patrick swallowed a bite of sandwich. "I know you want to go. It would be good to see them again, so go ahead and send a note that we will be there." Patrick had finished his soup and most of his sandwich.

"You shouldn't eat so fast," said Catherine. "It isn't good for your digestion."

He looked over at her and smiled, "So I've been told."

Patrick was busy finishing his chicken salad sandwich. "Your birthday is coming up. We can call this garden party a birthday party."

Catherine had finished her soup and took another sip of tea as she looked at him, her green eyes shining. "It's like killing two birds with one stone. And while we're mentioning my birthday, we could do with a new stove."

Patrick raised an eyebrow. "What's the matter with the one we have?"

"It's an old wood stove. Modern stoves are electric. I saw a lovely yellow electric stove in the *McCall's* magazine with three burners and an oven at the side. Mattie wouldn't have to bend over or haul wood."

Patrick smiled at his wife. "And I'm sure Mattie thought of this."

With a sheepish look, she replied, "Not exactly."

He offered a knowing smile. "Go ahead and make the arrangements. Perhaps the stove will be your birthday present and you can forgo the garden party."

That option hadn't occurred to her. "No," she replied, "we'll wrap it all up as the best birthday ever."

The time passed quickly. Patrick paid the bill with a healthy tip for Harry. They left the restaurant by the back door to avoid Lavinia Talley.

Patrick gave his wife a healthy kiss in the privacy of the covered back entrance, "I shall expect a sizable reward for my generosity."

Catherine's coy response came easily, "I promise you shall be rewarded twofold." After five years their romantic moments remained.

Patrick laughed and they went their separate ways.

On her way back home, Catherine was smiling to herself. The sky had become overcast, causing her to hurry as the darkening western sky looked threatening with rain. What if she got caught in the rain? After lunch with her husband, Catherine Burke had recovered from the morning irritation of burnt pancakes and spilled milk and drying children. She felt so giddy that a little rain wasn't going to dampen her spirits. But the sky was becoming ominous. The wind had started, the dark clouds forming with the sound of thunder in the distance.

Jean Marie was still playing with John Patrick while Carrie Jo and Mary Margaret were napping when Catherine arrived home. "Jeannie, you had better hustle on home because we're going to get a storm. Your mother will be worried."

"I guess I'd better. Mother says the thunder is the mighty hand of God slamming down when he is displeased with us mortals."

Catherine wrinkled her brow thinking that would be enough to strike fear in the hearts of vulnerable children. She wondered what the "holier than thou" Mrs. Moore said about lightning. She didn't ask.

Chapter 3

The next afternoon, Carolyn Thomas was sitting at Catherine's dining room table and eating a deviled egg that Mattie had included in their lunch. "Are you taking the children to Elizabeth's party?" asked Carolyn.

"I'd rather not," replied Catherine. "But, Mattie watches them when I need her to, and I don't think she's feeling all that well. Of course she won't admit it."

Catherine and Carolyn had gone through some trying times which made their friendship a tighter bond.

Ann Catherine, Carolyn's six-year-old, had been a difficult birth. It was Catherine who saw her through that trying time. And Carolyn had been there for Catherine when she suffered a miscarriage. The three of them, Catherine, Carolyn, and Elizabeth, who was hosting the garden party, had weathered the Great War together while their husbands served in the military. In fact, they had all gone to France to meet up with their husbands. It was a friendship circle never to be broken.

Carrie Jo and Mary Margaret were napping. John Patrick and Annie, Carolyn's daughter, were playing in the playroom, and Mattie was working in the kitchen.

Catherine's honey-brown hair was pulled back into a bun. She wore a plain housedress because she had been with the children all morning without time to change before Carolyn arrived.

They were drinking iced tea and eating finger sandwiches. "I'm getting a new stove for my birthday," said Catherine. "Do you think Asa could help me with ordering and delivering?"

Carolyn was slim and attractive and wore a high-necked white blouse and navy skirt. The outfit complemented her dark hair and brown eyes. She shrugged. "I'll ask, but you know my husband. Although he left the military, the discipline remains."

"I don't follow you, Carolyn. Asa is a gem."

"I'll put it this way. Everything is done by the book, and a kitchen stove doesn't fit into a farm store. He won't want to step on the toes of Mr. Coyner who could probably order it from his department store."

Catherine frowned. "I didn't think of that. I just thought that with Asa's store being next to the railroad tracks, it would be easier to get it delivered. The last thing I want to do is cause a problem."

She rose from her chair and went to the buffet. There, she opened a drawer and pulled out the picture she'd cut from the magazine.

Carolyn's eyes opened wide when she saw the yellow Peerless electric stove. "Oh, Catherine that will look perfect in your kitchen. Think of the space it will give you. What will you do with that one you have?"

Catherine chuckled. "The monstrosity that belonged to Patrick's mother? I'll give it to the first person who asks. I think Patrick just agreed to a new one because he won't have to look for a birthday present. Turning thirty seems a monumental milestone of some sort."

"It is," said Carolyn. "Lucky you, you'll be able to vote. I guess my work with the Suffragettes paid off." She hesitated a moment before she added "How do you feel about it?"

Catherine chuckled. "Do you mean about turning thirty or voting? I remember how Asa was against you carrying a right to vote sign and marching through the streets of Washington."

Carolyn sighed. "He believed in it. He just didn't like the idea of his wife being so bold."

"He was proud of you," said Catherine.

Carolyn was surprised. "How do you know that? He never said anything like that to me."

Catherine smiled. "Of course he wouldn't. I overheard him talking to Patrick."

Catherine and Carolyn were interrupted by Annie and John Patrick when they ran into the room, each carrying a glass canning jar. "Mama, Miss Mattie said we can go catch polliwogs in the fish pond if it's okay with our mothers."

"What do you think, Carolyn?" asked Catherine.

"It's all right with me, but Annie, you need to take off your shoes and stockings. I don't want those new shoes getting wet."

"And, John Patrick," said his mother, "It's the same for you. Take off your shoes and socks and roll up your trousers."

The smiles on the children's faces lit up the room as they peeled off their shoes and knee socks.

"What if I get my dress wet?" asked a concerned Annie.

"It's your play dress, it can be washed," replied Carolyn. "Just be careful that you don't fall in."

"Let's go, Annie," said John Patrick, and they were gone in a flash.

The mothers smiled as they watched them go before Carolyn looked at Catherine with a serious tone. "To get back to our conversation, I meant, how do you truthfully feel about turning thirty?"

"Truthfully?" replied Catherine. "I haven't had time to give it much thought, but I don't think it's going to feel much different than being twenty-nine."

Carolyn laughed and shook her head. "My practical friend," she said, "I have a few years before I hit that number, and I can honestly say that I am not looking forward to it. Don't ask me why, because I don't know. Perhaps it's the thought of becoming a dowdy old woman."

"You don't become a dowdy old woman at thirty," answered Catherine. "That is unless you allow yourself to become one. How did we get into this depressing talk, anyway?"

A cry came from upstairs, signaling that the little girls were awake from naptime. Catherine called out to the kitchen, "Mattie, Miss Carolyn and I will take care of the girls." She turned to her friend, "Come on, Carolyn, let's go up and put some spark in our lives."

Chapter 4

In the southern end of the county at the Red Gate estate, Elizabeth Caldwell was all agog planning the garden party. The thought of seeing her good friends again made her happy. If no one else came that would be fine with her. But, it was to be a big affair and it was important to invite important people. As with most gatherings, she expected guests would mill around the food tables then gravitate toward their own crowd as it seemed that was the direction most social events went. This was Elizabeth's first attempt at being the hostess of a large affair, and she wanted it to be perfect.

When the elder Caldwells were alive, Red Gate had been the scene of the Harvest Ball, a fete that was the highlight of the year. However, there had been no Harvest Ball since the war. Ruth Caldwell, the daughter, stepped in as hostess when her mother took ill. She was now married with a place of her own. Now the Red Gate estate was run by the two sons, Will and Andrew.

During the Great War, the farm had prospered as an army must be fed and provided livestock. War horses were needed, and Red Gate was a notable horse farm. Horses were bought and transferred to Fort Sill, Oklahoma to be trained. Andrew, Elizabeth's husband, was in the army during the war; Will remained at home to oversee the farm.

Elizabeth came from the Washington area and had owned Catherine's hat shop, which her parents had bought for her.

When she was eighteen and had a child out of wedlock, she was at death's door. Her parents, believing they had no alternative, had placed the baby in an orphanage.

The hat shop was to be a new start for Elizabeth, or was it to get her away from the stain she had brought on their name? For the young, blond, blue-eyed, pretty Elizabeth, the move to Clarke County was not to her liking. But she persevered. Meeting Andrew, although she didn't realize it at the time, had been a god-send. He helped her find her child, married her, and gave the child his name. Rumor had it that her first husband had died. That was also fine with Elizabeth.

Catherine, Carolyn, and Elizabeth's lives had intertwined, with their bond of friendship still strong. Isn't it interesting how different personalities and different ages can meld together?

Elizabeth knew Catherine was turning thirty because Carolyn had mentioned it when they talked on the telephone a few days earlier. Wouldn't it be fun to surprise Catherine with a cake when they came for the garden party, thought Elizabeth. On second thought, perhaps Catherine might be embarrassed, so she put the thought out of her mind. Elizabeth didn't want to do anything that might embarrass her friend.

Emily, Will's wife, called on her way from the house, "Elizabeth, Toby wants to know if you want the boxwoods trimmed?"

"Just anything that looks scraggly," Elizabeth called back. She saw Emily take a detour before she finally came to where Elizabeth stood.

Emily, petite and demure, came to Elizabeth with a light step. "Is there anything I can help you with?" she asked.

Elizabeth smiled. "I'm trying to map out where the best places are for serving food and drink at the party."

Emily's brow furled. "What kind of drink?"

"Lemonade and iced tea," responded Elizabeth.

Emily almost made an audible sigh of relief. She had her problems with alcohol and couldn't trust herself if there was alcohol within smelling distance. Married to the blustery Will, who tried to overcome his short stature with a pushy personality, it was no wonder that Emily had found solace in the bottle. Emily had been on the wagon since Elizabeth came, and she was always on guard that she didn't fall off.

"Do you think it would be nice to set the tables up under the trees," Emily questioned.

"That's what I was thinking," Elizabeth answered. "The trees would be a good shelter, and the leaves are not falling this time of year. We only have to be sure that the ground isn't sloping so the food doesn't slip off the tables."

"Perhaps Toby can find lumber in the barn for the serving tables. I'll ask Will if that would be all right," said Emily.

"Why do you have to ask Will? There shouldn't be any question about us using boards from the barn if we need them," said Elizabeth.

Emily scrunched her face. "Well, you know how Will is. He likes to be the one to give permission."

Elizabeth had a mind of her own. "If I need boards from the barn, I'll use boards from the barn. You know Andrew isn't going to balk. Good heavens, Emily, there are times when we need to stand up for ourselves."

Emily chuckled. "Of course there are, but I'll let you do the standing."

The remark made Elizabeth laugh aloud. "I guess I did sound a little self-righteous. Let's go to the hop kiln we use as a classroom. We can set that up in case someone feels faint or needs to lie down."

"That's a very good idea," agreed Emily. "We have that *Johnson&Johnson* first aid kit in there for the children's bumps and bruises. We'll just put in some smelling salts."

Emily and Elizabeth set out to put the little place in order. Clean sheets were put on the cot, an extra blanket folded and laid on a chest, and the medical supplies on the teacher's desk.

"Let's put a vase of flowers in here so it will really look like a sick room," said Elizabeth.

The quiet Emily laughed aloud. "I don't think you're overlooking a thing."

Elizabeth nodded. "I want this affair to be perfect."

Chapter 5

Catherine Burke's yellow *Peerless* electric stove was ordered from Kalamazoo, Michigan by Asa Thomas. He had talked with Mr. Coyner, but Mr. Coyner wanted no part in it because he had heard that sometimes those stoves came scratched or dented and would have to be sent back.

Where Mr. Coyner heard those words was unknown to Asa, but they weren't the words he wanted to hear. Dealing with farm equipment was one thing, dealing with a kitchen appliance was another. However, the Burkes were good friends, so he felt obligated. He called Catherine to tell her what Mr. Coyner had said. Catherine said she would take her chances.

It was nearing the date of Elizabeth's party when the stove arrived packed in a wood crate on the 5:15 train. A new electric stove all the way from Kalamazoo, Michigan was big news in Berryville. Asa's hired workers took great care in lifting it from the train onto the platform at his farm store. Looking through the slats, the color could be seen but not much else. Even the workers from the flour mill came across the street to peer in and get a glimpse of the *Peerless* stove.

Asa picked up the telephone and asked the operator to ring Catherine's number.

She answered the phone. "Catherine, this is Asa. Your stove has arrived. When do you want me to bring it over?"

"Oh, my goodness," said Catherine. "I didn't think it would arrive for a few more days. Mr. Lloyd wants my old stove for one of his tenant houses. I'll have to call him to see if he can pick it up tomorrow. Will that be all right with you, Asa?"

"See if he can pick it up in the morning, and we can deliver this in the afternoon. I'm not going to take it out of the crate until it's in your kitchen."

"Of course, I understand," said Catherine. "I'll call Mr. Lloyd right away and see what he can arrange." She hung up the earpiece on the phone with the intention of calling Buster Lloyd when John Patrick interrupted, "Mary Margaret needs her diaper changed. She stinks."

"That isn't nice to say," corrected Catherine.

"Well, she does."

"Where's Miss Mattie?" asked Catherine.

"She said she had to go home and lie down for a few minutes," answered John Patrick.

That was unlike Mattie, she thought, which sent a flash of concern through Catherine. But, Mary Margaret needed to be changed first, then she would call Mr. Lloyd, then she would check on Mattie.

Luck was with her when she called Buster Lloyd, and he said he could bring a couple of hired men and a flatbed wagon to pick up the stove early because he had plenty of farm work to do.

"How early is that?" asked Catherine.

"I figure 'bout six."

"That's fine," she agreed, although it would completely throw her day into a tizzy.

She called Asa right back to tell him he could come any time after he opened his store.

"I'll have to rearrange my schedule and give you a call before we come."

"I can't thank you enough," replied Catherine. She knew Asa was an organized man and to rearrange his plans for the day was no small gesture on his part. She would try to make it up to him, but she couldn't worry about that now, Mattie needed her attention.

She went to the playroom and changed Mary Margaret's soiled diaper. "John Patrick," she said. "I'm going to check on Miss Mattie. You stay in the playroom with the girls. I'll only be a few minutes."

"Can you take Mary Margaret? She keeps knocking down my house of blocks."

"Yes, I'll take her with me," Catherine said as she picked up her two-year-old. "Do you think you and Carrie Jo can play while I'm gone?"

"Carrie's playing with her doll house. Mary Margaret's the nuisance."

For a four-year-old, Catherine was proud of her son's vocabulary. However, calling his baby sister a nuisance needed correction. "You need to be tolerant of your sister, John Patrick. Tell her you're sorry for calling her a nuisance."

He looked at his little sister. "I'm sorry you're a nuisance," said John Patrick.

Mary Margaret was oblivious to the whole conversation. Catherine rolled her eyes and left with her daughter in her arms. She was just walking around the boxwoods when she almost bumped into Mattie, who was on her way to the big house.

"Mattie, I came to check on you. Johnny said you had to lie down."

"Got up too early, I be fine."

"I think you should talk with Patrick because that's unusual for you," said Catherine.

Mattie looked straight at her. "Don't you be tellin' Mistah' Patrick. There ain't nothin' wrong. Now, I need to get over and start fixin' supper."

Catherine knew it was no use to continue, but she was going to tell Patrick whether Mattie wanted her to or not.

She changed the subject as they walked back to the big house. "Mr. Thomas called and said my stove will be delivered tomorrow. Mr. Lloyd is going to pick up the one we have in the morning. He expects to be here around six o'clock."

Mattie stopped walking. "Now, how am I suppose' to feed my babies without no stove to cook on?"

Catherine had stopped also and turned to Mattie. "They can eat puffed wheat."

"That ain't no food for growin' children," said Mattie.

Catherine was not in the mood to argue. "I left the children in the playroom," she said as she hurried on and released some of her inner steam as she went.

That evening when Patrick returned from a hectic day at the Hawthorne House, Catherine was close to tears. "Oh, Patrick. I'm so glad to see you. I have had a terrible day."

Tired as he was, he took a seat in the parlor and asked, "What's the problem?"

"First of all, John Patrick is getting too big for his britches. Mary Margaret had an accident, and he said she stunk."

Patrick smiled, "She probably did."

"Then he said she was a nuisance because she kept tipping over his block houses. Then Asa called and said the stove is to be delivered tomorrow, and Mr. Lloyd is going to come pick up this one at six in the morning, and Mattie had to go home to lie down, and now she's mumbling to herself because she won't have a stove to use for breakfast."

Patrick held up his hand. "Whoa! What's this about Mattie having to go and rest?"

"Didn't you hear any of the rest of it?"

He sat forward in the chair. "Of course I did, but the most important is Mattie. What happened to her?"

Catherine had simmered down and came to sit in the upholstered chair next to him. "I don't know. When I went to check on her she was up and on her way over here. She didn't want me to tell you."

Patrick leaned back in his chair. "First of all, John Patrick is only four and a smart little guy. I'm sure he's heard those words used. It takes reminding of what's acceptable. As for the stove,

I'm happy it is here; that Asa will take care of the delivery and you will be rid of the one we have. I will talk to Mattie."

Catherine sighed. "You make it sound so easy. I guess I let myself get wound up like an eight-day clock."

Patrick rose from his chair, came to her, and pulled her to her feet. "I know it isn't easy, and I wish I could be of more help. Thad will be back tomorrow. I'll see if I can get home a bit early."

Catherine leaned her head into his shoulder. "That isn't necessary. It's just that I always had an orderly life, and I feel it is slipping away."

"No, love. You are now the mistress of a large house, my wife, and the mother of three precious children. It is not easy, and you do a wonderful job."

"Patrick, I'm worried about Mattie."

"So am I." He kissed the top of her head. "We'll have supper, get the children into bed, and I'll go over and have a talk with Jacob and Mattie."

Catherine tipped her head up and kissed him. "You seem to make everything right."

Chapter 6

The next morning Catherine was up at five o'clock to make coffee and prepare for the removal of the kitchen stove. She cooked up some ham and eggs for herself as Patrick had said he would leave early and have breakfast at the Berryville Hotel.

At six o'clock, as promised, Buster Lloyd arrived with three hired men. The clattering of the wagon as it came up the drive to the back of the house probably woke all of Church Street, thought Catherine. However, she was delighted to see them and was eager to get that monstrosity of a stove out of her kitchen. It would give her time to clean up the room before Asa brought in the new stove. Some sweeping and mopping, and all would be back to normal before noon.

Catherine had the door open. "Come right in, Mr. Lloyd," she called when she heard his steps on the gravel path.

He stepped inside and tipped his work cap, "Good mornin', Mrs. Burke."

"Good morning," she answered.

He stood admiring the black iron stove decorated with ornate brass-colored leaves. "That sure is a pretty thing," he said. "I might have to change my mind and put it my house."

Catherine couldn't see any beauty in it and rather than agree, she replied, "It is yours to do with as you please."

He went to the door and motioned to his helpers to come inside. The three burly fellows and the skinny but wiry Buster Lloyd stood eyeing the stove.

Buster stood with a hand on his chin. After a moment, he said, "I figure once we unhook the flue and take out the burner covers, we're gonna 'have to turn it on its side to get it out the door. How'd they bring it in Miss Catherine?"

Catherine had been standing to the side watching. It took her a second to respond. "I'm not sure. I wasn't here when they brought it."

"You got a yardstick?" Buster asked.

Catherine went into the sewing room and brought the measuring stick to Mr. Lloyd.

He clicked his fingers together. "Shoulda' thought to bring one," he mumbled to himself.

They went about measuring the stove and the doorway and decided they would have to remove the door to get the stove out of the kitchen. There was a toolbox on the wagon. Two of the men started removing the door, while Mr. Lloyd and the other hired man began dismantling the metal flue. As soon as they unhooked it, a cloud of black soot went flying everywhere.

Catherine's eyes flew open and her hands went to her face. "Oh, my goodness!" For the second day in a row, she felt close to tears.

"Boy, that's a mess," said Buster, standing there with black soot covering his hat and shirt.

When Catherine recovered, she said, "I'm sorry. I guess that should have been cleaned before you came."

"That don't make no never-mind," he answered and smiled at her,

Catherine's teary feeling turned to irritation as she watched them track soot all over the kitchen floor. When they finally got the stove out and loaded onto the flatbed wagon, Patrick, having heard the commotion, came tripping down the back stairs, dressed in his three-piece suit, ready for a day of treating patients. He stopped on the last step when he saw what had happened.

In a jovial mood, he said, "I see Buster got the stove."

As much as she loved her husband, there were times… Catherine threw a dish towel in his direction. "Go to work, Patrick, but I suggest you take the front stairs."

"How are you going to clean this up? I hate to leave you with it."

"I'll bet," she answered with irritation in her voice.

Somewhat penitent, Patrick offered, "I'll stop over and see if Jacob can come and help." Before Catherine could reply, he was on his way to the front stairs. Patrick knew when it was time to leave.

Catherine was sitting on a kitchen chair surveying the damage when she heard John Patrick's voice. He was standing in the doorway between the kitchen and dining room. "What happened, Mama?"

She looked over, smiled at her son, and in a calm tone said, "Don't come in, sweetheart. It was an accident when Mr. Lloyd came and took out the stove."

"It looks awful," he remarked.

"It is awful," replied Catherine. "I have to get it cleaned up before Mr. Thomas can bring our new one. Are the girls awake?"

"No."

"Good. Be quiet and don't wake them. You can stay in your night clothes until they get up. Are you hungry?" asked Catherine.

At that moment, Jacob appeared at the open kitchen door. "Miz' Catherine, Doctor Burke said you might need my help, an' from the looks of this place, I sure think he's right."

"Hi, Mr. Jacob," called John Patrick, "Ain't that a mess?"

"Isn't that a mess?" corrected his mother, still sitting on the wooden straight chair.

"It is for a fact," said Jacob. "Why don't you go on over to our place so Miss Mattie can give you breakfast whilst I help your Mama put this place straight?"

"Is Mattie feeling all right?" said a concerned Catherine.

"Yes, ma'am. Sputterin' a bit about her babies not gettin' a decent breakfast. She's makin' grits and gravy."

"Oh, boy!" exclaimed John Patrick. "Can I go over, Mama?"

"May I go, and yes, you may. Miss Mattie won't care if you show up in your sleep clothes."

John Patrick was out the front door in a flash.

"I hate to ask you to help with this, Jacob," apologized Catherine, "but it has to be done, and I can't do it by myself before the girls are up."

Jacob gave her a big smile. "Don't you worry none. We'll make this kitchen sparkle before you get that pretty new stove."

Jacob was off to gather cleaning supplies when Carolyn appeared. "Patrick told me about the accident, and I came to give a hand," she said.

This time tears did fill in Catherine's eyes. "Oh, Carolyn. I am so glad to see you. I feel like my orderly life is falling apart."

Carolyn had seen John Patrick on his way to Mattie's and sent Annie with him. She entered the kitchen, skirted the sooty places, came and gave Catherine a big hug. "No, dear friend," she said, "your life isn't falling apart."

"What is the matter with me? I have always been so in charge."

"It's because you're turning thirty."

Catherine made a sour face. "What's that got to do with it?"

Carolyn shrugged. "I don't know. Maybe you have another baby on the way," she said.

Catherine's eyebrows flew up. "Perish the thought!"

"At least I took your mind off the mess we are about to tackle."

"Did Patrick stop by on his way to work?" asked Catherine.

"He did," replied Carolyn. "He said you threw a dish towel at him."

"I threw it in his direction. Carolyn, it is not like me to act like a two-year-old. I'll apologize when he comes home. I don't think I've ever been so upset."

Carolyn offered a sympathetic smile. "That's understandable. I really think Patrick was amused by the whole thing."

Catherine sighed. "He probably thinks that's justice for wanting a new stove."

"And, by the way, Asa was still home when Patrick stopped in. Asa said he will wait to hear from you about delivering the stove. I can hardly wait to see it."

"My enthusiasm is waning," said the beleaguered Catherine.

Jacob appeared with rags, brooms, mops, and buckets. "Mattie says she can make some stew for your supper on our stove," he said.

Carolyn jumped into the conversation before Catherine could reply. "That's kind of Mattie," she said. "However, the Burkes will be coming to my house for dinner."

"Carolyn that isn't necessary," said Catherine.

"Nonsense," replied Carolyn. "What are friends for?"

That afternoon when Asa had delivered the stove into the thoroughly scrubbed kitchen, he said, "Catherine, you need to call G.T. before the stove can be hooked up."

"Can't you just plug it into the socket?"

"I believe it might take some extra wiring," replied Asa.

While they were talking, his hired man was taking down the slats of the crate that held the prized stove. Every removal of a slat brought an "ooh" and "ahh" from the bystanders when they saw the gleaming yellow porcelain coming into view.

With eager anticipation, crowded around in the kitchen and watching the process were: Catherine, Carolyn, Annie, John Patrick, Carrie Jo, and a skeptical Mattie with Mary Margaret in her arms.

"That's a right pretty piece," said the hired man after he and Asa had placed the stove in the spot of the previous heavy iron wood stove. John Patrick and Annie ran over to run their hands over the smoothness.

"Holy sh…sh…sugar!" said an excited John Patrick. "It feels like glass."

"Children, take your hands off the stove," admonished Catherine. "And, John Patrick. Where did you hear that expression?"

"From the men who took out the old stove."

This brought a grin from Asa as he wondered if the crusty farm hands had used a different expletive, and John Patrick was smart enough not to repeat it. Asa, the former military man with a commanding presence, held a soft spot for John Patrick.

Asa brushed a lock of dark hair from his forehead. "You're right, J.P., it is as smooth as glass." J.P. was a pet nickname Asa used for him, and John Patrick liked it because it made him feel grown up.

Chapter 7

The next morning Catherine had been waiting for Mr. Thomas to arrive. Hearing his knock, she went to the door and ushered him in. "Good morning, Mr. Thomas. I'm glad to see you."

G. T. Thomas was pleasingly plump, in his late forties, and dressed in overalls. "Hear you've got a new electric stove," he said.

"Yes, sir," answered Catherine. "I believe the whole town knows it."

G.T. chuckled. "Probably so," he said.

"Asa said you needed to check it out before we could hook it up."

Mr. Thomas went right to the new appliance and looked it all over. He opened the oven door and found a packet of instructions. He pulled out the papers and said, "Hmm. Looks like you're going to need a heavier line."

"Heavier line?" said a puzzled Catherine. "What does that mean?"

He answered. "If you plug into that socket, you'll be shooting fuses like Fourth of July fireworks."

Catherine furrowed her brow and swallowed hard. The cost of her stove was going up. But, the problem had to be solved, so she cleared her throat and said, "If it has to be done, how soon can you fix it?"

"Can't get to it today," he replied, "but I can be here first thing tomorrow morning."

"That will be fine. Thank you for coming." What else could she say?

He shook his head. "Got a busy day ahead," he remarked, and G.T. Thomas ambled out the door.

Catherine felt like the wind had gone out of her sails. She would feed the children puffed wheat, whether Mattie agreed or not, and they would have a cold supper. On this rainy day, they could turn their cold supper into a picnic and have fun in the process.

When Mattie appeared after Mr. Thomas had left, Catherine told her she was giving her the day off. Mattie said she didn't need no day off, but Catherine insisted. She wasn't going to put up with Mattie grumbling to herself all day because of the stove.

She telephoned Carolyn. "Carolyn, why don't you and Annie come over and spend the day? It's such a gloomy day. The children can play in the play room, and we can sit and knit or crochet or embroider or whatever you want to do. Play cards, play checkers…"

"You certainly are down," said Carolyn. "I'll pack up some stuff and be over within the hour. Annie will love to spend the day in the playroom."

When she arrived, Catherine told her what G.T. said. Catherine added, "I don't know how much it's going to cost."

"If I know Patrick," said Carolyn, "that's not going to bother him a bit."

Catherine shrugged, "I'm sure it won't, but it makes me mad."

"Why? You're getting what you want. You should be pleased," said Carolyn.

"That advertisement should have said that it may need some extra wiring," said the irritated Catherine.

"It should have, but it didn't, and that's the way they sell the goods. Would you still have bought it if you had seen that you couldn't just plug it into any socket?"

Catherine smiled. "Yes, but I would have been prepared."

"Then quit griping," said Catherine's best friend. "Where's Mattie?"

"I gave her the day off," answered Catherine. "Much to her disagreement."

"Tell her you changed your mind so she can watch the children. We can take Carrie and Mary Margaret with us and see what Irene Butler has in her dress shop. I want to find something pretty for Elizabeth's garden party."

"It's raining. I'm not going to drag those little ones out in the rain."

"Good point," said Carolyn. "Let's wait until naptime, and we can go then. Annie and John Patrick can play in the playroom while we're gone."

Catherine shook her head. "No. I am not going to tell Mattie I changed my mind."

"Then I will," said Carolyn, and out the door she went.

Catherine did not even mention a word of protest. It would be very nice to spend some time in Irene's dress shop to lift the disquiet of the past couple of days, thought Catherine.

Chapter 8

The walk in the light rain to Irene Butler's hat shop on Main Street was exactly what Catherine needed. Carrie Jo and Mary Margaret were napping, Annie and John Patrick were having fun in the playroom, and Mattie had come as Catherine knew she would.

If Mattie held a grudge, it didn't show, and Carolyn's sunny personality, even on a rainy day, could charm anyone.

They walked with umbrellas although the rain had turned to mist, and chatted, as friends do, on their way down Church Street then west on Main Street to the shop. The pudgy Irene was her usual negative, gossipy self, but that didn't dampen the spirits of the two looking for just the right outfit for the party.

The new dress styles were straight with dropped waists, below the knee and adorned with lace. They were light, airy and soft to the touch: fine cotton and wool, silk, linen, georgette.

All manufactured dresses in the shop would look perfect on the slender Carolyn. It was a different story for Catherine as she was bustier and round in the hips. The optimism of the day was beginning to dim.

"I can make a dress for you, Catherine," said Irene. "I have your measurements, although it looks like you've put on a few pounds." Tact was not one of Irene's strong points, but she made up for it as she was an excellent seamstress.

"That garden party is the buzz all around. Lavinia said she and Jeremy would be there to cover the highlights of the day," informed Irene.

Carolyn, who had been viewing the readymade dresses, turned her head and smiled. "I'm sure they wouldn't miss it."

Irene ignored her and continued working with Catherine. "I'm sewing a design for Ruth Bass. You remember her. She was Ruth Caldwell before she went to England and met that Captain Bass. After all, she grew up on Red Gate, and I used to make her dresses for the Harvest Ball. Guess this garden party takes its place," said Irene.

"Of course I remember her," said Catherine.

"That young woman's changed, although Ruth is still picky about what she wants," continued Irene. "Maybe she needs to outdo Elizabeth." Irene shrugged her shoulders. "Lavinia says Ruth and Elizabeth didn't click when Elizabeth owned your old hat shop, Catherine."

Catherine knew Irene was fishing around for her to say something about Ruth. She had been an unfavorite customer when Catherine owned the millinery. Catherine smiled to herself when she remembered that she used to call her "ruthless". But that was never to anyone but herself. The wise Catherine wasn't going to give Irene the satisfaction of being pulled into her gossip trap.

"The party is only a couple of weeks away. Will you have time?" Catherine asked the seamstress.

"Once you pick out the material and the pattern, I can start it next week.

What about you?" asked Catherine, turning to Carolyn "Have you found one you like?"

"I like the trim yellow linen." She held it up for Catherine and Irene to give their opinions.

There was no question that the dress would look captivating on the attractive Carolyn.

Catherine fingered the crepe georgette. "Does this come in peach or teal?"

"Same as the color of the duck," laughed Irene. "Maybe a shade lighter. I've got a bolt in the back room if you want to see it."

By the time they left the shop, Catherine had ordered a dress without the dropped waist but with a higher waistline that accentuated the bust and slimmed the hips. Irene said it would be ready for a fitting by Friday of the next week.

When they left the dress shop, the rain had stopped. Catherine's mood had lifted, and she gave Carolyn a quick hug. "You knew what I needed," she said. "I have been so busy I hadn't even thought of what I would wear."

"Wasn't that fun? Let's walk over to Josephine City. There's a milliner there who creates the most glamorous hats. We might even find a scarf to go with our new clothes," said Carolyn.

Before they headed up Church Street, Catherine said, "Let's go to Coyner's department store. I want to buy Mattie a treat, and they have the most wonderful candy counter."

"Feeling guilty?" asked Carolyn.

Catherine chuckled. "You know me too well, but Mattie deserves a reward just for being Mattie."

Carolyn nodded.

Nettie was behind the dry goods counter when they went into the store. Nettie was around twenty and had been married as soon as she finished high school. She was on her way to replace Lavinia Talley in the nosy department.

"Miss Catherine and Miss Carolyn, how nice to see you. What can I help you with?"

"I came to buy some candy," said Catherine.

Nettie tripped over to the candy counter. "We have a wide variety. These chocolate drops arrived this morning." Of course, they were the most expensive aside from the boxed chocolates.

"I was thinking of an assortment of the hard candy," Catherine said, thinking of the added expense of the cost of the stove.

With a condescending smile, Nettie said, "Yes, they're down at the end with the cheaper candy."

Yes, thought Catherine, you're going to fit perfectly into Lavinia's shoes.

Catherine offed half a pound of her order. "Have you heard about the big garden party at Red Gate?" Nettie asked while she was weighing the candy.

While Catherine was keeping Nettie busy, Carolyn was strolling around to see what new merchandise had arrived since she was in the store last.

Catherine answered, "I've heard about it. I understand it will be a lovely affair." Nettie stopped short of asking if she was going. However, Catherine knew that Nettie knew that she was good friends with Elizabeth and would be attending. And if she didn't, Irene would tell Lavinia, and Lavinia would tell Nettie.

"I'm sure there will be a nice write-up in the *Courier*," said Catherine.

"I suppose," said Nettie. "The candy will be ninety-eight cents."

Catherine handed Nettie a dollar bill which she put in the canister that hung on a cable. She zipped it up to Mr. Coyner, whose office was on an elevated platform off the stairs leading to the second floor.

Mr. Coyner dropped two pennies into the canister and zipped it back to Nettie. Nettie removed them and handed the change to Catherine.

Carolyn came to where Catherine stood. She held a pair of tan gloves in her hand. "What do you think, Catherine? Will these go with the linen dress?" She slipped the fine lace trimmed glove on one hand.

"I don't think you could find anything better," said Catherine.

They waited while Nettie and Mr. Coyner went through the same routine and left the store with a thank you to Nettie and a wave to Mr. Coyner.

When they returned to the house, Carrie Jo and Mary Margaret were up. John Patrick and Annie had a full afternoon of play, and Mattie was feeding the four of them graham crackers and milk at the kitchen table. The *Peerless* stove stood like a silent sentry.

Catherine's outlook had improved one hundred percent from the gloom of the morning. Mattie was delighted with her candy, although she was not one to gush her pleasure.

Tomorrow, Mr. Thomas would hook up the stove meaning only one night of a cold supper. Things were looking up at the Burke house.

Chapter 9

The next morning G.T. Thomas, with tool box in hand, arrived at eight-thirty. Catherine greeted him at the kitchen door and invited him in.

"A bit muggy out there," he said as he opened the tool box. "As I remember it, your fuse box is down in the cellar."

"I guess so," Catherine answered. "Patrick takes care of blown fuses, the few we've had."

"Yes, ma'am. This house is wired right." He chuckled. "I know because I wired it."

Catherine had to smile. She wanted to say that if he'd thought ahead, the heavier line would already be installed, but she didn't.

It took the whole morning of Mr. Thomas going up and down the cellar stairs before he came to where Catherine was sitting at her secretary's desk finishing a list of supplies she needed at the general store.

"I'm ready to plug her in," said G.T. "Want to come watch?"

Of course she did. However, the first thing she did was to go upstairs to find Mattie. She was changing sheets on John Patrick's bed.

"Mr. Thomas is ready to plug in the stove. Do you want to come down and watch?"

Mattie looked at Catherine with an expression of "do you have any more silly questions?"

She dropped the sheet on the bed and followed Catherine down the back stairs to the kitchen where the magic was about to be performed.

"Now, ladies, if this works the way it's supposed to," said G.T., "this here coil is going to start with a pink glow and turn to red. That there's what they call the cooking element." He turned a switch on the front of the stove.

Catherine and Mattie watched with wide eyes as they saw the pleasant glow Mr. Thomas had described.

"You turn the switch to regulate the heat. The more you turn it to the right the hotter it gets." He turned the switch off before he tested the other burners and finally got to the oven.

"This here's pretty fancy," he said. He pointed to a round object next to the oven door. "It's called a thermostat and works like a thermometer. You can set it to the heat you want with this switch." He showed them the fourth switch on the front of the stove. "That's all there is to it. Mind you, if you forget to turn off the switch, it's going to burn up anything left on top, so you got to remember to turn off the burner. And, if you put something on and turn on the wrong burner, it ain't going to cook. You got to be careful with the kids. They like to fuss with the switches, so keep them away so they don't burn themselves, 'bout the same as with a wood stove."

When he finished his dissertation, he said, "Got any questions?"

"It looks easy enough," answered Catherine. "I guess it will only take some getting used to. What do you think Mattie? You'll be the one using it the most."

Mattie didn't say a word, she just stared at Catherine with a disgusted look. G.T. was quick to pick up on the friction in the air and hurried to say, "Most of the new cook books tell you what temperature to set it at for pies and cakes and that sort of thing."

"I don't use no cook books," said Mattie.

G.T. scratched his head. "Wal' now. That might pose a problem."

"We'll work it out," said Catherine as she was not going to get into a prolonged discussion about using the stove. "Mattie and I will use trial and error if need be."

Mattie frowned. Trial and error weren't going to help her put a decent meal on the table.

When Patrick arrived home from his day of treating patients, Catherine was all abuzz over the new stove. "It's wonderful," she told him. "Mattie can cook three things at once, and when she gets used to the oven, she'll find it so much easier."

Patrick thought it wise to get Mattie's opinion, but he didn't want to dampen his wife's enthusiasm. "I'm happy it's taken care of," he said. "Did G.T. leave a bill?"

Catherine winced. "He did. I put it on your desk."

"From the look on your face, I'm not even going to ask how much it cost."

"Good" she replied. "I wouldn't want to ruin your supper."

Chapter 10

Josephine City was a self-sufficient black community located off South Church Street, which had been bought by former slaves and freemen from Ellen McCormick, owner of Clermont farm. The town consisted of 40 acres and became an oasis for black citizens of Clarke County.

Mattie and Jacob attended the Zion Baptist Church, and Mattie bought their groceries from the grocery store in Josephine City, but they preferred their quaint house close to Catherine and Patrick. After all, they were brought up in the city and just like the story of *The Country Mouse and The City Mouse*, there is a difference in their upbringing.

The morning Catherine and Carolyn approached, the milliner, Charity Jackson, answered their knock and led them into the room in her house that was used to create her hats. Charity was in her thirties, a slim black woman with a welcoming smile.

"Good morning, ladies," she said. "Please have a seat."

"Good morning," they answered as they each sat in a straight-backed wooden chair. "I assume you received my note about what we are looking for," said Catherine.

"Oh, yes ma'am. Billy delivered it on Tuesday. I have some ideas for you to look over. As

I understand it, Miz' Carolyn, you have a yellow linen outfit, and Miz' Catherine, you have a bluish-green georgette."

"That's right," said Carolyn. "I bought a lovely pair of tan gloves, which I've brought with me to see if you can match something up." Carolyn removed the gloves from the box she carried.

The milliner threw up her hands with excitement. "Miz' Carolyn, I think I've got some lace someplace that will match the trim on your gloves. But first we need to decide on the style. If you're goin' to be outdoors, I believe a wide–brimmed straw would be a good choice." The milliner clearly knew her way around in the millinery business.

"What about the Musketeer hat? I've seen pictures of them in magazines," said Carolyn.

"Don't you think those hats are a bit too lavish for Clarke County?" asked Catherine.

Carolyn looked over at her. "You mean I'd look like I was showing off?"

"You could put it that way," said Catherine.

The milliner smiled. She knew Catherine had owned a hat shop, and Catherine also knew who the haughty women were who could get away with wearing a Musketeer hat. So did the milliner.

"I have a straw that would closely match your gloves, and I can trim it with lace and flowers to bring the outfit together. Would you like to see it?" asked the milliner. She was interrupted by a knock on the door. "Excuse me ladies," she said as she went to answer the knock.

Catherine and Carolyn could hear the conversation.

A child's excited voice said, "Mama wants you to come on over 'cause Grandma's pretty sick, and she didn't know what to do."

"I can't come right now. What's the matter?"

"She's throwin' up and got the runs. Cain't keep nuthin' down," said the anxious young girl.

"You run on home and tell your momma I'll come soon as I can." She closed the door and went back to her customers. "I'm sorry, ladies," apologized the milliner.

"Was that Grace Page's little girl?" asked Catherine.

"Yes, ma'am, my niece," replied the milliner. "My mother's taken sick."

"I can have my husband come," offered Catherine.

"No, I'll go over later," the milliner was quick to reply, and too proud to say they couldn't pay for a doctor.

"We don't want to keep you," said Carolyn. "I am a nurse. I would be glad to look in on your mother."

"I know and I thank you, but I think she jus' needs some tending to. My sister is quick to get a worry."

There was no more said about the sick lady, and they were delighted when they left the milliner's house, happy to have their outfits ready for the big affair. Carolyn's hat was a pancake straw to be trimmed with lace and flowers, and Catherine's was a taller, wider-brimmed white straw that would be fancied up with tulle and feathers the color of her dress.

On their way home, Catherine said, "I'm going to ask Patrick to go and check on her mother once he gets home. It doesn't sound good that she's been sick for a few days. The granddaughter sounded very upset."

"Yes, she did," agreed Carolyn "I wish Miss Jackson would have let me go check on her. I will gladly pay for a house call."

Catherine shook her head. "You know as well as I do they aren't going to accept that. Patrick has a way with words, so I am in hopes they will allow him in. He will do it out of the goodness of his heart."

They reached the Burke house and Carolyn continued on down the street to her house. It had been a fruitful morning.

Mattie's helper was cleaning the upstairs, and Mattie was feeding the children lunch when Catherine walked in the front door.

"I'm proud of you, Mattie. You used the new stove to make the chicken soup. It smells good. Is there enough for me?"

Mattie gave her a broad smile. "Plenty of soup, Miz' Catherine. And, I didn't have no trouble with that stove."

"When are you going to start using the oven? I'd love an oatmeal cake."

"Soon's I ain't afraid of that thing you turn," answered Mattie.

"We'll work on it tomorrow," said Catherine. She unpinned her hat while Mattie put a hot bowl of chicken soup on the table so Catherine could join her children for lunch.

When Patrick arrived from his day at the office, Catherine told him about Mrs. Jackson. Without hesitation he said, "I'll go on over right after we eat."

Chapter 11

When Patrick arrived at the Page house, he removed his hat and said," "Good evening. I'm Doctor Burke. My wife told me that Mrs. Jackson is not feeling well, and that I'd better hurry over here or I wasn't going to get any dessert for my supper." Grace Page smiled and opened the door for him to enter.

Both daughters, Grace and Charity, were with Mrs. Jackson when Patrick arrived. They didn't protest Patrick's presence and took him to where their mother lay on a cot. She was a big woman and lay almost lifeless under a clean white sheet.

"How long has she been sick?" Patrick inquired.

Grace Page, the older of the two and a big woman like her mother, spoke. "Momma lives with us, and a couple days ago, she said she had a stomachache, I gave her some baking soda in water. She said she felt better, but that night she threw up. Now she cain't keep nothin' down and she's got the runs. She's about wore out."

"Yes," agreed Charity, "I came over the next morning and gave her some chicken broth." She added with a shy smile, "I live two houses away. I'm making a hat for your wife, Doctor Burke."

Patrick smiled at her. "And, my wife is pleased. Did your mother keep the broth down?"

"For a spell," answered Grace. "It was today she's been losin' from both ends."

Patrick took out his stethoscope from the doctor's bag he carried. He examined the woman, who had been silent except for a few moans and groans. Then he turned to the two concerned daughters. "Do you have any of the broth left?"

"Yes, sir," said Grace. "There's some in the ice box."

"Good," said Patrick. He took a bottle and spoon out of his bag. "I'm going to give her a spoon of this and hope it stays down. In fifteen minutes we'll will try with a few spoons of your chicken broth."

He didn't say what the alternative was if she continued as she was.

"Grace, you go clean up from your meal, and I'll heat up the broth," offered Charity.

The two women left the room, and Patrick gave Mrs. Jackson the medicine. He wiped the perspiration from her brow with a cloth that sat on a stand by the bed.

"Mrs. Jackson, I'm Doctor Burke. Do you hear me?"

A weak raspy voice said, "I hear."

"I know how badly you feel, but I expect you will get better if you take the medicine that I'm going to leave with your daughters. It doesn't taste too good, but it's the only way you're going to get better, so I want you to tell me you'll take it."

She nodded.

"Good enough," he said. He sat back in the straight chair and waited for the medicine to take effect.

Charity opened the door and entered with a bowl of chicken broth and a spoon.

"Give it to her in slow spoonfuls once it cools down. I'll be back to check on her."

"Yes, sir," said Charity.

Patrick left the room and found four young faces looking at him. They were quiet as mice. Patrick gave the worried faces a big smile. "I think your Gramma's going to be fine."

"Doctor, I'm giving the children milk and a piece of apple cake. Would you like some?" Grace asked.

"Now, that sounds just fine," said Patrick.

They made space for him at the crowded table, and the quiet-as-mice children came alive with conversation and laughter.

Once Patrick finished his cake and thanked Grace, he went back into the little room to check on his patient. Charity was sitting by the bed. She rose when Patrick entered.

"I've given her a few spoonfuls as you said, so far it's stayed down."

"Good," he answered. "If someone can give her a sip of water and spoon of broth every hour, you should see some improvement by morning. If not, you are to summon me. Otherwise I will stop by tomorrow evening after I get home."

When Patrick left, Mrs. Jackson had kept down the broth, and he had left medicine and instructions for Grace and Charity. "I'll be back in two days unless you have a problem, and you can send one of the children to my house."

Catherine was waiting for him when he arrived home. "How did it go?"

"I believe it is one of those stomach bugs, and I think our lady is going to feel a lot better in a couple of days. I'll know tomorrow if it is something more serious. I had a delicious piece of apple cake Grace Page made. Mattie should get that recipe."

Catherine came over and kissed his cheek. "You know that isn't something Mattie is going to do. She's still fussing about using the stove and won't touch the oven. But, she's learning in spite of herself. Tomorrow I'm going to work on using the oven. I found some recipes that came with the instructions for using the stove. She'll sputter and mutter, but if it works to bake a cake, she'll come around. Why don't you put your bag away and we can go on up to bed."

He grabbed her around the waist and pulled her into a hug. "I can't think of a more enticing idea."

Chapter 12

Harry West was sitting at a desk in the back room of the Battletown Inn opening the day's mail. In the mail, he was surprised to find a fine linen envelope addressed to him. He was more surprised to find an invitation to a garden party hosted by Andrew and Elizabeth Caldwell at Red Gate, an estate in the south end of the county. He was welcome to bring a guest or two.

Elizabeth had enclosed a note:

Dear Harry,

I am sending this invitation to your work place as I am unaware of your mailing address. You have been such a congenial helper when we have frequented the restaurant that we would be pleased to have you come to Red Gate.

We look forward to seeing you.

Elizabeth Caldwell

Harry smiled to himself and thought, does this mean I have arrived? And, he smiled again. The party was not quite two weeks away. Would there be time? He could send a telegram to Washington, but he couldn't take the chance of sending it from Berryville. The telephone would be the same problem. Harry, the articulate and impeccable waiter, decided to send his usual monthly letter early. If all worked out he would take a guest to the garden party. Of course, he knew the clerk at the post office would make an off-hand remark about the letter being early. Harry knew an answer wasn't necessary. He would just nod and give a half smile before he left the post office.

Harry put the invitation in his coat pocket. It was time for the lunch patrons to arrive. He straightened his bow tie, polished his silver belt buckle, ran a rag across his shined shoes and checked himself in a mirror that sat in a corner of the room. The customers would expect an impeccable waiter and he wasn't going to let them down.

Chapter 13

It was a drizzly rain, but undaunted, Lavinia Talley raised her umbrella the minute she stepped out of her house on Main Street. She hustled on up to Irene Butler's dress shop as quickly as her round body would allow and walked into the shop. Irene was in the back room working on Catherine's dress.

Lavinia rushed into the room without a "good morning". "Irene I heard that Irish girl who lives at Lockwood has left her husband and gone back to Washington."

Irene looked over her glasses with perspiration on her brow. "Wipe my forehead with that rag," she said as she nodded toward the piece of material. "I need to finish this tricky spot."

Lavinia obliged the seamstress. "What are you working on?" she asked.

"Catherine Burke's dress for that party down at Red Gate. Are you going?" said Irene. That was idle talk because she knew very well that Lavinia and Jeremy would be going, although Lavinia confessed they hadn't received a formal invitation.

"Oh, I wouldn't miss it. Jeremy and I received the invitation a couple of days ago. Have you been invited?"

"Not to my knowledge," answered Irene.

"It's supposed to be the biggest affair since they had to give up the Harvest Ball during the war." Lavinia was all atwitter. "I'm sure Catherine will look lovely, although she has put on a few pounds since having all those children. She certainly did a complete turnaround since marrying that doctor."

"Well, I think I'd turn around for him, too," said the seamstress. "So what's this about Fannie leaving Jess Edwards? Now there's a man for you." She bit the thread with her teeth and laid the dress on the worktable. "You want a cup of tea?"

"That would be nice," said Lavinia.

Irene had the water hot in an enamel tea kettle on a one-burner kerosene stove. She put a tea bag in each cup, poured the water, and handed a cup to Lavinia. "Let's go sit over at the little table."

The two heavily endowed women took their cups and sat on the two straight chairs with a small table between them.

"Herbert Marks said he took Fannie Edwards up to the Bluemont station so she could get a train to DC. He said she looked sad and her husband wasn't with her." Lavinia clicked her tongue and shook her head. "I just don't know about that woman."

"Who told you she was leaving him?" asked Irene.

"Well, no one did, but it's as plain as the nose on your face; otherwise her husband would be with her."

"You never liked her," said Irene. "Is it because she's an outsider?"

"Of course not! I am very open-minded," said an indignant Lavinia. "She doesn't have the reserved good manners of her friend Adelaide Lockwood. I don't understand why they became such close friends."

"I understand Fannie was a great help to Adelaide when she worked in Washington," said Irene.

"Maybe," said Lavinia, "but I'd just as soon that she and Jess stayed out in California when they went out there. Neither one of them were born in Clarke County." Lavinia sipped her tea.

"You're right," said Irene. "Do you want to see Catherine's dress before it's finished?"

"Of course," Lavinia answered. "There is nothing like a sneak peek."

"Don't go blabbing it all over town," said Irene.

Lavinia frowned. "I'm insulted."

The two town gossips knew each other well.

Chapter 14

Mattie was determined to learn how to use the oven on the new *Peerless* electric stove. She was mixing up the batter for a pound cake when Catherine came into the kitchen carrying Mary Margaret. She took off her diaper and sat the child on the wooden potty chair, then gave her a ginger cookie to eat while she sat.

"I'll be glad when she's out of diapers," Catherine said to Mattie. "I remember when I had three of them in diapers all at one time. It seemed like all I did was change diapers and feed."

"She's learnin' right good. Seems girls are easier than boys," said Mattie. "Our little Johnny was always havin' accidents."

Catherine shook her head and smiled at the memory. With Mary Margaret settled and happy, she turned to Mattie. "I've read the instructions for using the oven, Mattie, and it doesn't sound too complicated. Do you want to try to use it?"

"I guess. I'm fixin' a pound cake for supper 'cause Mistah' Patrick ain't had no dessert for over a week."

"Yes he has," said Catherine. "He had a piece of apple cake Mrs. Page made, and he said you should get the recipe from her."

"I can make apple cake," said Mattie without a smile.

Catherine ignored her. "First we need to know what temperature we need to bake the cake. Do you have any idea?"

Mattie looked at her with a blank stare. "I put my hand in the oven and feel if it's hot enough. Then I know how much wood to add," she answered.

Catherine shook her head. "That isn't going to work. The instructions say that most cakes bake at three hundred and fifty degrees." She went to the stove and looked at the thermostat. "All I have to do is set this dial to the three hundred and fifty mark." She turned the dial. "Now we wait for it to heat up."

Mattie watched with narrowed eyes and didn't say a word.

"You go ahead and finish mixing your cake and pour it into a pan. I'll see to Mary Margaret, and keep an eye on the oven."

Catherine picked up her child and checked to see if she was successful. Then she gave the toddler a big kiss and said, "Aren't you a big girl!" The toddler was pleased with herself and gave Catherine a soggy ginger cookie kiss.

Catherine took Mary Margaret to the play room and returned to the kitchen. She announced with a happy voice, "Look Mattie. This light comes on when the oven's ready. Isn't that remarkable?"

Mattie wasn't so sure, but she held the pan of batter while Catherine opened the oven door. "Go ahead," said Catherine, "put the pan on the middle shelf."

Mattie did as she was told. "Now it says to time it," said Catherine.

Mattie wrinkled her nose. "Time it?"

"Yes, to judge when it's done."

"I jus' guess and stick a straw in it when I think it's done," said a wary Mattie.

Catherine shrugged. "I guess you can still do it that way. But, isn't this wonderful and so much easier than that old wood stove?"

"Guess we'll know when the cake comes out," mumbled Mattie.

Catherine said a silent prayer. Thirty minutes later, her prayer was answered when she pulled a perfect cake from the oven.

Chapter 15

Three days later, Catherine and Carolyn went to Charity Jackson's millinery to pick up their hats. Charity answered their knock and escorted them into the room she used for her millinery business.

"It's nice to see you ladies," she said. "I'm right pleased with the way your hats have turned out. You'll look good and proper for your party."

The young women smiled as they took their seats. "How is your mother?" asked Catherine.

With a broad white-toothed smile, Charity replied, "She's doin' much better. Jus' needs to get her strength back. That medicine Doctor Patrick gave her was what she needed. It was kind of you to send him."

"He was glad to be of help," said Catherine and she thought 'Doctor Patrick' must mean he was accepted.

Charity brought two hat boxes from a corner of the room. "Doctor Patrick told Grace that you have a newfangled stove."

Catherine and Carolyn both laughed.

"Yes we do," answered Catherine. "Our Mattie was reluctant to use it, but once she got over the skittishness, she's been baking up a storm. My husband said that he had a delicious piece of apple cake that Mrs. Page made for him."

That brought another wide smile from the milliner. "Grace likes to cook. I'm not good at it, but I only have to cook for myself." Perhaps that explained the difference in the physical appearance of the two sisters.

Charity took out Carolyn's hat first. Carolyn jumped up from her chair with a burst of glee. "It's beautiful! I can't wait to try it on."

"You come right over here and sit in front of the mirror, Miz' Carolyn."

Charity placed the pancake style hat at just the right angle on Carolyn's pretty dark hair. "I was right about the lace trim," said Charity. "It matches the trim on your gloves, and the tulle will blend in to bring out the color of your outfit."

Carolyn turned to look at Catherine. "What do you think? Will I look classy for the garden party?"

Catherine chuckled. "You'd look classy any place."

Charity was busy taking Catherine's hat from the taller box. "It's your turn Miz' Catherine."

Carolyn vacated the chair in front of the mirror so that the milliner could place the straw hat atop Catherine's honey-brown hair. It was a wide-brimmed white straw that she had trimmed with feathers and a side silk ribbon and streamers down the back.

"You said your dress was a shiny teal color, Miz' Catherine, so I did my best to bring it all together."

Catherine took the milliner's hand. "And did it better than I could have."

Charity let out a sigh of relief. "It makes me proud for you to say that. I know you were the best around."

Catherine released the milliner's hand and smiled at herself in the mirror, remembering Mary Lee Thompson, the local young woman who worked for her. It was Mary Lee who had the creative edge, thought Catherine.

Charity repackaged the hats in their respective hat boxes. She refused to allow Catherine to pay for the hat. "It is repayment for Doctor Patrick taking care of my mother."

Catherine didn't protest as it would be a breach of politeness.

They left the millinery with Charity waving at them from her doorway. "I'm getting more and more enthused about this affair," said Carolyn as they walked down Josephine Street. "How about you Catherine?"

"My life has been such a hub-bub for the past week, I haven't had time to think. But, yes, I am looking forward to it. I want to leave the girls at home and take John Patrick, but I don't want to burden Mattie. She doesn't say anything, although I've caught her sitting and resting. I'm going to talk to Patrick again."

"What about Jean Marie Moore?" suggested Carolyn. "Perhaps she could watch the girls while you're gone. Mattie and Jacob would still be there."

"Jeannie said she was going to the garden party with her parents. I need to take some quiet time to sort out my thoughts," said Catherine. Then she chuckled. "Finding quiet time at my house is almost impossible."

Chapter 16

When Adelaide Lockwood received the invitation to the Caldwell's party, she almost jumped for joy. She hurried out the back door of the stately manor house to find Alex and tell him the good news.

He was talking with his foreman, Caleb Dunn, and his irreplaceable hired man, Jess Edwards, the man whose wife supposedly left him according to the stories flying around the town of Berryville. The three men stopped talking as Adelaide came up to them.

"Hi Addie," said Caleb and Jess in unison.

"Good morning," she said.

"What is it Adelaide?" Alex asked. He was patient, but Addie wondered if she had intruded.

"Alex, I didn't mean to butt into your conversation." She felt her face flush and said, "I wanted to tell you that we've received an invitation to the Caldwell's garden party."

The three men looked at each other and smiled.

"I believe that could have waited until later," said Alex.

Addie, embarrassed and not wanting to look like a complete fool, answered in an authoritative voice, "The sooner I get your answer, the sooner I can respond. I believe the Caldwells will appreciate it."

Alex smiled at her. "You may tell them we will be pleased to attend."

Addie turned without a word and started back to the house, but she was sure she heard some snickers as she walked away, and the men resumed their discussion.

Addie's husband, Alexander Lockwood was fifteen years her senior, so wasn't it likely that he would not share in her enthusiasm? He had been a notable lawyer in town before he married her. He gave up lawyering to handle the estate he had purchased and appropriately named it Lockwood. The vast acreage was north of town and sat on Clifton Road. With a stately columned porch, the white manor house was perched on a knoll with a full view of the Blue Ridge Mountains in the distance.

Adelaide had attended Kathcrine Gibbs, a business school for women. She kept the books and all the other paperwork that went into keeping the place running. Her upbringing had been in a tenant house. Wasn't it natural that she would be excited to be considered one of the landed gentry? She penned a reply to go out in the next mail. That wasn't enough to quell her delight. She had to share the news with someone and that someone was Lottie Bell.

Addie's best friend through her school years and through an adventuresome trip to Leadville, Colorado was Lottie Bell Foster. She was now Lottie Bell Dunn, the wife of the foreman at Lockwood.

Lottie, Caleb and their three children lived in a brick tenant house at Lockwood. It had been almost five years, and Caleb was due to be given fifty acres to start building a farm of his own. Those were the arrangements when he agreed to leave Colorado, where he and Lottie met.

Lottie and Addie were still dear friends, but their lives had taken different paths. Lottie never left Clarke County once she returned.

Adelaide had taken a position with the Red Cross in Washington during the war. It was in D.C. that Addie met Fannie Quain. They became roommates and close friends. It was Addie who introduced Fannie to Jess Edwards.

Those memories popped into Addie's mind as she sat in a state of bliss. How fortunate she had been to be in the position she was now. And, how fortunate she was to have her two sincere friends living on the estate.

The rumors about Fannie leaving Jess had reached her ears, but she paid no heed as she knew Fannie had been called to Washington to care for her ailing mother. Let the gossips have their day, just as they had when Alex married her. Fannie would be back, but would she and Jess get an invitation to the Caldwell's affair? Probably not, just as Caleb and Lottie wouldn't. Adelaide rose from her chair, neatly arranged the papers on her desk and left the house to have a talk with Lottie.

The three Dunn children were playing in the front yard when Addie arrived. They stopped their play and ran to her. "Hi, Miss Addie, Momma's inside," informed Cal, the oldest of the three, who, like Catherine Burke's children, were a year apart. The difference was that Lottie almost died with the birth of her third.

Addie hugged all three of them before she heard Lottie call from the doorway, "Come on in. I'm about to take bread out of the oven."

"Yummy," called Addie. "Do you have a cup of tea to go with it?"

"I suppose I can manage that," said Lottie as Addie came onto the front porch. "What brings you here in such a happy mood?"

"How do you know I'm happy?" asked Addie.

"The way you almost bounced down the path. I saw you coming from the kitchen window." Lottie turned and Addie followed her into the kitchen where the aroma of fresh bread whetted her appetite.

"You and Fannie make the best bread. Do you make those kigleys like Fannie does?" asked Addie.

"I've tried," answered Lottie. "I don't make them as good as she does. Have you heard from her?" Lottie was getting two mugs from the cupboard.

Addie said, "This is according to Jess. He said that he got a letter from her the other day. She expects to return in a week. Her mother is better, she's tired of the city, and she can't wait to get back."

Lottie poured hot water over the tea bags in the mugs and put them on the table before she cut two slices of warm bread. "Do you want some honey for your bread?" Lottie asked.

"Got any of your yummy strawberry jam?"

Lottie smiled. "I just made a batch. Here, I put what was left into this dish. You can spoon it out."

"Got any butter?" said Addie.

"Gads, Addie. You're a hard woman to please."

"No, I just want to get the most out of your delicious bread." Addie buttered her piece of bread and spooned the fresh strawberry jam on top. "Ah, this is the life," she said when she took her first bite.

"That's because you didn't have to stand over a hot stove and put all the labor into it," responded a practical Lottie.

While they sat enjoying their repast, Addie said, "Alex and I have been invited to a garden party at the Red Gate estate."

"So that's what put the spring in your step. I knew there had to be something big to put that wide smile on your face," said Lottie. "I suppose you're all worried about what you're going to wear to fit in."

Addie took a sip of tea. "I haven't had time to think about it, although the thought has crossed my mind that I will be one of the youngest wives there and will most likely feel out of place."

"You know some of the women who will be there. Maybe your Aunt Lilly will attend. She owns that big Roseville farm down in Boyce," said Lottie.

Addie looked over at her and smiled. "I didn't think of that. I'm acquainted with some of the other women, but it's not like being with you and Fannie, and I'm sure Fannie won't be going."

"Like I won't be going," said Lottie.

"I don't mean it to sound uppity, Lottie. If I wasn't the wife of Alex, I wouldn't be going, either. You know I love to get dressed up, and I can't do it around the farm," countered Addie.

Lottie smiled at her. "I know. Maybe we're such good friends because we're so different. Going to a lavish garden party would not appeal to me in the least, and I don't think Fannie will be disappointed. When is the party?"

"It's about two weeks away. Do you want to ride into town tomorrow? I should go to Irene Butler's dress shop to look for an outfit," said Addie.

Lottie thought for a moment, the offer was tempting. "I can't leave the kids," she said.

"I'll have Peg come and watch them. We have another girl who comes to help a couple times a week. One of them can come." Addie's mind worked at a quick pace when there was something important she wanted.

"I would like to get out of the house for a change. And, I'll be tied up with the gardening before long." Lottie was good at reasoning. "What time do you want to leave?"

"We'll leave at eight. I'll have Jess get the buggy ready," said Addie.

"As soon as Peg shows up, I'll head to the house," responded Lottie. "I haven't been to town in over a month."

Addie's enthusiasm was back. "We'll have a great time. Just like we were teenagers again."

Lottie shook her head. "I don't want to go through those years again."

Chapter 17

Elizabeth Caldwell was sitting at her secretary desk in the den at Red Gate. She was going over the list of invitees and the responses she had received.

Andrew spied her as he passed the den to go out the back door. He stopped, rapped on the open door before he stepped into the room. "You look pretty, and hard at work," he said as he kissed her cheek and took a seat in the straight chair beside her desk.

"Good afternoon," Elizabeth said. "I'm trying to get an estimate of those coming so that we will have enough food."

"And tables and chairs," said Andrew. "The older I get, the more I like to sit."

Elizabeth looked at her husband and laughed. "You're not even thirty, and still the handsome man I married. I noticed you limping more last evening. Is your leg bothering you?"

"This old war injury is a nuisance." He slapped his leg. "It seems to ache more on rainy days. How is the party coming? You've put a lot of planning into it."

Elizabeth sat back in her chair, ran her hands through her blond curls, and stretched her arms above her head. "I hope it doesn't rain. I couldn't cancel at the last minute."

Andrew's handsome face lit up with a smile. "We could move it up to the ballroom. Since we haven't had a Harvest Ball that big room is going to waste."

Elizabeth chuckled. "It's going to storage. Have you been up there lately?"

He shook his head but got an idea. "Want to go up and check it out?"

"Oh, I can't, Andrew. I have to finish this."

"Come on," he said. "We'll both take a break and go exploring."

She hesitated a moment before she said, "All right. I could use a change for a few minutes."

Andrew was out of his chair and stood by her side with his hand extended. "Madam, may I have your hand? We shall go adventuring."

Elizabeth laughed aloud. "Kind sir, I will follow you anywhere." And when she rose from the chair, she reached up and gave him a lip-smacking kiss.

Hand in hand, they left the den and went up the winding stairway to the third floor ballroom.

He opened the door and let out a whistle. "You weren't kidding. Who put all this junk up here?"

"It's not junk," said Elizabeth. "It's still useful. Look, over there is that monstrosity of a commode with the steer horns that came from Texas. And your old bed leaning against the wall…"

"Where's the old Victrola?" said Andrew as he looked around the huge room.

"Probably where it always was," answered Elizabeth.

Andrew went around a tall dresser and chest of drawers. "Here it is," he called.

Elizabeth went around the bulky furniture and sure enough found Andrew with a record in his hand. "Let's see if it still works," he said as he wound the handle, lifted the lid, and dusted off the record with his handkerchief before placing it on the turntable.

A scratch sound was heard before they recognized the notes of *The Blue Danube* waltz. He looked at Elizabeth and grinned like a school boy. "Let's dance."

Elizabeth giggled and went into his outstretched arms. "We haven't danced in a long time."

Around the furniture and knick-knacks, to the open spots they could find, the two waltzed as though they had been to a ball the day before. Even the limp in Andrew's injured leg didn't slow him down.

When the record ended and the scratchiness returned, they came to the Victrola where Andrew picked up the arm and slid the lever before closing the lid.

"That was wonderful," said Elizabeth.

Andrew put his strong arms around her and pulled her to him. They stood entwined in the silence of the large room, enjoying the closeness and forgetting the outside world until Andrew murmured in her ear, "I suppose we have to get back to the real world."

Elizabeth sighed. "I love you, Andrew Caldwell. Even if this garden party turns out to be a big flop, I know I can cry on your shoulder."

He smiled as he released her. "No, my love. It will be a gathering to remember."

Hand in hand, they tripped down the back stairs where Andrew gave her a quick kiss before he headed out to the horse barn, and Elizabeth went back to her guest list. When she finished, she would go down to the kitchen to check with Ollie about the food. Ollie, the cook, had worked for the Caldwells for many years. The kitchen was her domain and she let everyone know it.

Chapter 18

Catherine Burke, after a hectic day with the children, decided that she would take John Patrick to Elizabeth's party. She would find someone to help Mattie with the two little girls, as she did not want to spend the afternoon at the party by having to keep an eye on them. She wanted to spend the time talking with her friends. Their days of a good gabfest were too few and far between.

Was she being selfish and inconsiderate? The thought did cross her mind. She knew Carolyn would agree with her, and Carolyn was looking for someone acceptable to help Mattie with the children. At least, that was what Catherine understood when they talked about leaving the girls at home. Catherine would pose the problem to Patrick when he came home. Meanwhile, she had to go into the playroom to settle some dispute over a toy or Mary Margaret destroying something of John Patrick's. Carrie had learned to play with her brother, but not so with the two-year-old. Like any child of that age, what was hers was hers and what was anyone else's was also hers.

When Patrick arrived that evening and the children were in bed, Catherine told him of her decision.

Patrick was reading the *Washington Post* newspaper. He put it down to look at her as she sat across from him working on handwork. "What do you think?" she asked. "Do you agree it would be all right to leave them with Mattie? I haven't even mentioned it to her."

"It's good that you haven't. I had a long talk with Jacob the other day. I think Mattie has a heart problem from what he's told me. Thad can handle the office tomorrow. I'm taking the day off. I plan to sit her down and get to the bottom of it."

Catherine let her handwork drop in her lap. "You didn't tell me."

"No. I want to be sure before it sends your world in an upheaval. We will have to decide what she is capable of as far as taking care of the children and this house."

"I'm not too surprised, Patrick. She isn't going to want to hear about relinquishing her responsibilities," said Catherine.

"Of course I know that," he said. "But she will have to understand if changes are to be made."

Catherine shook her head. "Good luck on that. She may listen to you; I know she wouldn't listen to me."

"I'll take care of it tomorrow," said Patrick and he went back to reading the news.

Catherine put the embroidery piece in her work basket and rose from her chair. "I'm tired," she announced. "I'm off to bed."

"I'll be up in a few minutes," he said. "I want to read what's going on with Wall Street."

Catherine checked in on her sleeping children before she went to her bedroom. John Patrick, the spitting image of his father, was wrapped in a ball of sheets and blankets. In the next room, her sweet, blond-haired Carrie Jo was fast asleep, and in the crib was her dark-haired toddler Mary Margaret. She wasn't a baby anymore, which gave Catherine a twinge of regret. She left the door ajar when she left to go to her room.

In her and Patrick's bedroom, she sat in front of the mirror on her dressing table and brushed through her long hair. Maybe she should get it cut in a new style like Carolyn's. No, she thought, it's easier to wind it up in a bun. As she looked in the mirror, she noticed she looked tired, and there were tiny wrinkles beginning to show around her eyes. She wondered what tomorrow was going to bring, if Patrick determined that Mattie had to curtail most of her duties regarding the house and children.

A determined Catherine decided she would face whatever the days ahead brought. She didn't need any more complications in her life. After all, she was close to turning thirty. Didn't anyone understand that? Catherine Burke let out a big sigh as she laid the hairbrush on the dressing table. She didn't like this melancholy mood that had snuck up so quietly.

Then she heard Patrick's step on the stair and smiled. His presence had a way of vanishing the blues.

Chapter 19

Adelaide Lockwood and Lottie Bell Dunn arrived in the town of Berryville before noon. Irene Butler was busy with all sorts of sewing paraphernalia strewn around the work room in the back of her shop on Main Street.

"Good morning, Mrs. Butler," sang Addie as Irene came into the shop area.

"Good morning, Adelaide," replied the seamstress. She turned to Lottie. "Well, hello Lottie Bell. I could use your help. I'm swamped what with this big to-do down at Red Gate."

Those were not the words Addie wanted to hear because she wanted Irene to sew an outfit for her. Before Lottie could return the greeting, Addie said, "Does that mean you can't sew a dress for me to wear to that big to-do?"

"Don't see any way I can," answered Irene. "I've got some nice ready-made outfits."

Lottie knew Addie had her heart set on a hand-sewn outfit of her design. "Mrs. Butler, I wish I could help you out, but with the three children and a house to take care of, I really don't have the time."

"Too bad," said Irene. "You're a good seamstress."

Coming from the not-so-likable Irene, Lottie took it as a compliment. She had worked in the dress shop when she finished high school, and although Irene taught her more than she'd learned in Home Economics, the woman was not easy to work with.

Addie's attention was on the rack of manufactured dresses, while Lottie and Irene discussed the woes of dress making. Then Lottie said the words she hoped she wouldn't regret, "Mrs. Butler, do you have any material for sale?"

The seamstress frowned at her. "You know I don't sell my material."

"I thought you might have some end bolts you might like to part with."

Addie caught that part of the conversation, turned, and looked at her friend. What was Lottie up to?

Irene hesitated, then said, "Come on out back. I might have something."

Addie left the rack of clothing and followed the two to the back room. "My goodness," said Lottie when she saw the disarray of the work area. "I surely wish that I could lend a hand. The important ladies love your work." A little flattery went a long way with Irene, especially if it was true.

The seamstress took time to look at the bolts of material lining the bottom shelf. "You can look through these. You know they have less expensive material down at Coyner's."

"Yes, I know, but I'd like a dressy outfit," replied Lottie. "Addie come and help me pick out something."

There were only eight to choose from, but there was a pink silk and lavender lace with enough material for what she wanted. Lottie whispered to Addie out of earshot of Irene, who had gone back to her work, "Have you got enough money to pay for this?"

"What are you going to do with it?" Addie whispered back.

"I'm going to make your dress."

Addie looked at her with surprise before she took a roll of bills out of her pocketbook and handed it to her friend.

Lottie removed the bolts from the shelf and took them to Irene. "I'd like these two."

Irene looked at her with a wary eye. Lottie was pleasingly plump. "You sure there's enough material left on them for what you want?"

"As long as I'm careful when I cut out the pattern," answered Lottie.

Irene removed the material, measured it, and charged handsomely. Lottie never blinked an eye, paid the price with Addie's money, and thanked the seamstress.

Out on the street and away from Irene's view, Lottie handed Addie's money back to her. Addie said, "She charged too much. You know she isn't going to use that material or she wouldn't have sold it."

"You want a special outfit for that garden party, don't you?"

"You know I do," said Addie.

"Then don't complain, and let's go to Coyner's to pick out a pattern and whatever else I need," said Lottie.

Addie smiled. "All right. Let's go see if nosy Nettie is working at Coyner's."

When they stepped into the department store, there were a few other customers, which was good news for Addie and Lottie. They went immediately to the sewing section and found a pattern that would work well with the material they had purchased. Lottie matched the right color thread, picked up a card of pearl buttons and a card of hooks and eyes. Addie took them to the counter and waited for the customer ahead of her to receive his change, which Nettie pulled from the canister that had been zipped up to Mr. Coyner. He sat in his office off the stair landing where it was a perfect spot to observe the entrance door and the first floor.

"Hello, Adelaide," greeted Nettie. "I haven't seen you for a while."

"No," said Addie. "I am quite busy at Lockwood. Lottie and I got the chance to come into town for some shopping and lunch."

"That Irish woman, Fannie, isn't with you?" asked Nettie. She sounded like a young version of Lavinia Talley.

Addie knew Nettie was fishing around for fodder to feed the stories going around. Sorry Nettie, thought Addie, you're not going to get any information from me. "No, Mrs. Edwards is out of town."

Nettie smiled that 'I know the real story smile', but didn't push it further because there was another customer waiting.

Addie thanked the clerk, picked up her package, and she and Lottie left the store.

"What did Nettie say?" asked Lottie.

"She asked if Fannie was with us, and I told her she was out of town. Fannie should be back soon and quell the rumors circulating."

"It'll blow over," said Lottie, "especially when there's something else to talk about."

"I suppose," said Addie. "Let's go to the Battletown, and I'll buy you lunch before we head back."

"I want to go to Mr. White's general store before we head home," said Lottie.

"Do you want to go before we eat? I have a few things I need there, also. I hope we don't run into Mrs. Talley."

"So do I," said Lottie. "We've seen Irene Butler and nosy Nettie. That should be enough punishment for one day. No wonder I don't come into town more often."

"I think we need to eat, Lottie. You sound sour." Addie shifted her package to her left arm, slid her hand through Lottie's, and the two friends were off to the Battletown Inn.

Harry West greeted them. "Good afternoon, ladies. I have a table for two by the front window." He led the way and seated them both. "It's a lovely day out there," he said.

"Yes it is," replied Addie. Lottie nodded.

Harry placed the menus before them. "May I get you something to drink while you are deciding on your lunch? We have a special today of vegetable soup and an egg salad sandwich."

"That sounds perfect," said Addie. "What do you think, Lottie? Should we settle on that?"

Lottie was not one to complain or get edgy unless she needed to eat. Addie thought the sooner Lottie ate, the better it would improve her disposition.

Addie smiled at the affable waiter. "We'll take the special and a pot of hot tea."

"A good choice," said Harry West as he picked up the menus.

It was a good choice because the tea, soup and sandwiches came after a short wait.

"I'm starved," admitted Lottie. "I wonder what they have for dessert?" Lottie liked her sweets.

Midway through their meal, Harry came to check on them. "May I bring another pot of tea?"

"No, thank you," answered Addie. "This is fine. What do you have for dessert?"

Harry smiled. "Wonderful cream puffs, apple pie, and a light custard pudding"

Lottie didn't hesitate. "I'll have the cream puff." It seemed the food had renewed her good nature.

"And I'll have the custard," said Addie.

When Harry brought the desserts, he nodded toward the package Addie had placed next to her chair. "I see you young ladies have been shopping," he remarked.

"Yes," said Addie. "We came into town to have a dress made at the dress shop, but the seamstress is too busy."

"I've heard that she is sewing for some of the ladies attending a garden party. Word does get around."

"Does it ever," said Lottie as an off-hand remark.

Harry gave a knowing smile as he had been the recipient of many words that got around.

Addie chuckled. "Most likely the same garden party I'm going to down at Red Gate."

Harry put their used plates on the tray he carried. "Perhaps I shall see you there," he said. Then he whisked away the tray and left the ladies to their desserts.

Harry West was invited to the party? Addie raised an eyebrow and looked across the table at her friend. Lottie shrugged and dug into her cream puff. "What a wonderful way to end our lunch," she said.

Addie smiled over at her. "I don't think buying your lunch is going to repay you for making my dress."

"It won't," Lottie replied. "You can buy me some chocolates at the general store."

Their next stop was the general store where Mr. White remembered them from their young growing up years. He still gave them a free candy stick: peppermint for Addie and root beer for Lottie.

Chapter 20

Mattie listened to Patrick, although she didn't agree with him. "I know you think you're doin' what's right, but it ain't right."

They sat talking in her kitchen. Jacob stood by the sink. "It's just for a few weeks," said Patrick, "until I see if the medicine is going to help. I'll get a couple of women to help while you rest up."

Mattie shook her head. "I ain't gonna' lay around here all day. I know just the way Miz' Catherine likes things."

"I don't mean for you to lay around like an invalid," countered Patrick. "You can still help over at the house, but no heavy work. I'll talk with Catherine. We can come up with a list of what you will be allowed to do."

Mattie frowned. "I don't want no women takin' care of my babies or messin' with my stove."

Patrick smiled. It appeared the *Peerless* stove had become hers. He knew Catherine would be pleased to hear that after the complaining Mattie did when the old wood stove was hauled away.

Jacob spoke up. "Mattie, you need to listen. It's only for your own good. You know you ain't ben' feelin' right for a spell."

Mattie's mood had not improved. She frowned at her husband. "I ben' doin' all right," she said.

Patrick rose from his chair and took a bottle of pills from his bag. "You need to take one of these pills once a day. It's to help regulate your heartbeat. I'll want to check in a few days to see if they're making a difference. Meanwhile, pay attention to your husband and Catherine. You're a stubborn lady Mattie, and I love your stubbornness and all."

That brought a smile to her face. "We ben' friends a long time, Mistah' Patrick."

"That we have," he replied. "You come over to the house tomorrow and have a talk with Catherine."

Jacob followed him out of the little house. "I hope she does as you say," he said to Patrick.

"If she follows orders and the medicine helps, she should do fine. She isn't going to be able to assume all her duties, you understand."

Jacob nodded.

Patrick went in the back door where he found Catherine busy in the kitchen.

"I'm almost afraid to ask how it went," she said.

Patrick shook his head. "It's as I suspected. She's got heart problems. I've given her a form of digitalis. I'm in hopes it will help, but she isn't going to carry on as she has in the past. I've talked with Mattie and Jacob. They understand the medicine is to prevent a heart attack, and Mattie has agreed to follow my orders. Now, I want to sit down with you and devise a list of what she will be allowed to do."

Catherine turned from the stove where she had put on a pan of potatoes to make a potato salad. "You do realize I depend heavily on Mattie."

He nodded. "I do. That's why we've got to figure out what we need. I've told her that we will have to hire a couple more women."

"I'll bet that set well," said Catherine.

Patrick smiled. "She doesn't want anyone else to take care of her babies or 'mess with her stove.'"

This brought a chuckle from Catherine. "She gave me such a hard time over that stove."

Patrick set his bag on a straight chair. "Do you have time to sit and talk about this?"

"Jean Marie is in the playroom with John Patrick and Carrie. The baby is still napping," replied Catherine. "I have some time before these potatoes are ready."

"You must remember Mary Margaret is no longer a baby. Children need to grow," he cautioned.

"I know. I think she will always be my baby," said Catherine with a nostalgic tone to her voice.

Patrick winked at her. "Or until another one takes her place."

"Don't even let that thought enter your mind," she said. "Let's go into the dining room and try to figure out how I am going to replace our Mattie."

"Not replace her, dear. Lessen her activity."

"And find competent women to do her work? Carolyn and I have both been racking our brains to find someone to care for the girls. I don't want to take the girls to Elizabeth's party, which is next week, and I can't even figure how I'm going to manage that." Catherine's irritation with this turn of events was beginning to show. Patrick sensed her frustration.

"It'll all work out," he said.

"Perhaps."

She tried to smile, "You want a glass of tea?"

"Something stiffer may be called for," he said. "But tea will do."

The strained look on Catherine's face faded away, and she went to the kitchen for tea.

They sat at the dining room table. It soon became apparent that they needed someone to do the laundry, but Mattie could fold and put the clothes away. She could dust, but not mop the floors.

They would have to hire a cook. Mattie could help with cleaning up the table and drying the dishes after someone washed them, and she could still help feed and dress the children.

The list was sensible. It would keep Mattie busy enough, and she would be allowed to supervise any hired help, whomever they would be.

It was then that they heard Mary Margaret, and there was no Mattie to go up and get her. Catherine started to rise.

Patrick put his hand on her arm. "I'll go," he said. "You sit here and give some thought to our problem."

Our problem, thought Catherine, I do believe it will be my problem.

Chapter 21

At the Red Gate estate, Elizabeth Caldwell was in the downstairs kitchen with the cook, Ollie and her husband Toby. Toby had worked at the farm for years.

"Toby, are you sure we have enough tables and seating places?" asked Elizabeth.

"Now, Miz' Elizabeth, don't you fret about that. You tol' me there's be about fifty people, so I've had the men put together benches and chairs. We've even painted them white, just like you said. We've put up two tables for food and a big long table for the tea and lemonade. We can chip a block of ice that mornin' an' keep it in the ice house."

Elizabeth clasped her hands together. "That sounds perfect." She turned to Ollie. "Do you have enough help for serving, or do I need to try to find a few ladies."

"Miz' Elizabeth, it ain't good for you to get all wound up about this. We all have taken care of the big harvest parties we used to have. This is just like movin' it outdoors."

"I guess," said Elizabeth, "but I wasn't around for those balls. I want this to be as grand and enjoyable as those were."

"You can be easy knowin' we've done what you wanted," said Toby.

"Thank you," said Elizabeth. She left the kitchen to find Emily, whom she found in the former hop kiln turned into a one-room school/first aid station for the garden party. "I just talked with Ollie and Toby," Elizabeth informed. "They say they are prepared. Have you talked with the musicians?"

Emily finished placing towels and washcloths onto a dry sink. She turned to Elizabeth. "I had word from them yesterday. They are a trio of classical musicians, but one of them also plays the fiddle in case we need something livelier."

Elizabeth smiled. "Toby said they have built a platform for them. He hopes to set it up in a couple of days. We only have five more days. What about the flowers? I almost forgot."

"I have Mrs. Green working on that. She's talented at decorating with fresh greens and flowers. I think we are in good shape," said Emily. "Will has griped about using too much lumber, but that's Will."

Elizabeth nodded. "Andrew says whatever we want is fine as long as he doesn't have to be involved." Elizabeth and Emily both knew Andrew was out grooming and supervising the stables, as he wanted to show off his prize stock of horses.

"How can two brothers be so different," Emily said as a statement. "Have you heard from Ruth? I have to remind myself that she was the favored and coddled one who grew up here."

"Finally," answered Elizabeth. "She and Preston will be coming. Why do you think it took her so long to respond?" Elizabeth wondered.

Emily sat in the caned chair by the cot they had prepared in case of need. "I don't know. Once she returned from England after the war, and then married her English sea captain, she keeps her distance."

Elizabeth sat on the cot. "She has changed for the better. Perhaps the memories of her time here aren't pleasant, or she doesn't want Preston to hear stories. What do you think of Preston?" asked Elizabeth.

"I find him charming," said Emily.

"So do I." Elizabeth smiled. "Maybe Ruth wants to keep him all to herself."

Emily snickered and shrugged. "Maybe. I believe she was very fond of James Anderson when he worked here, but, and this is between you and me, I think James was fond of Carolyn Wilson when she came to care for Mrs. Caldwell."

"You mean Carolyn Thomas," corrected Elizabeth.

"Yes," said Emily. "She was Carolyn Wilson when she came to work here. In fact, she was the one who helped me climb out of the bottle."

"Don't belittle yourself. It was your way of coping with Will. I know you have to guard against it, and I'm proud of you for setting your life straight."

"You know, Elizabeth," said Emily, "you and Carolyn are the best things that have ever happened here at Red Gate."

"If it wasn't for Andrew, I wouldn't be here. He is the best thing that has ever happened to me.

I've never stopped loving him, even through those irritable, depression days when he returned with his war injury that ended his career in the military."

"May I tell you secret?" asked Emily.

"Only if you want to."

"I've never told anyone this," her voice dropped to a whisper, "I didn't want to marry Will."

Elizabeth felt her jaw drop.

"My parents said it would be a good match as I would always be provided for. We were not up to the status of the Caldwells. I met Will at a friend's birthday party. He was some kind of shirt-tail relation of my friend. Will wasn't popular with his own set, but he liked me. Andrew, on the other hand, could have any young lady he wanted."

"Did you marry to please your parents?" asked Elizabeth.

"Partly. Will was nice, affectionate and courteous. Sure of himself. I was eighteen, the shrinking violet. His real personality came out after we were married for a while. I think he has always been jealous of Andrew," Emily confessed.

"He has no reason to be. Will is smart, sometimes overbearing, but he keeps this place on even footing," said Elizabeth. "Probably better than Andrew could."

Emily smiled. "It has worked out for us. I believe since I've straightened out my life and gained some backbone, Will respects me for it. I'm no longer an embarrassment to him."

"Will loves you, Emily. Unfortunately, he is not one to say it," said Elizabeth. "I see it in his actions."

Emily nodded. "I know he does, and after a few rocky years, I have no regrets that I married him. I think we've grown wiser together."

"Isn't that what marriage is? Two people who weather the storms and triumphs as one, all the time growing stronger in the process?" said Elizabeth.

Emily laughed. "You put it so well. How did we get into this conversation anyway?"

"By sharing a secret that will never leave this little school house of ours," said Elizabeth. "We all have a skeleton in the closet. Now, it's time to go to the house and check our list for the party. I think we are in good shape. That is, if it doesn't rain."

Emily rose from her chair, and Elizabeth smoothed the covering on the cot before they left for the manor house.

Chapter 22

It was Monday of the garden party week. Catherine and Carolyn were to go to Irene Butler's to try on their outfits to see if any altering was needed. Jean Marie had come to play with the children. The woman who helped upstairs was there, and Catherine said she would pay her extra if Mattie needed the help.

Mattie was to sit in the playroom while Catherine was gone. Sitting did not appeal to Mattie, so she had a bushel of green beans to snap until Catherine returned. Annie was also in the playroom.

Catherine felt somewhat comfortable, as there appeared to be enough supervision.

"You worry too much," said Carolyn. "Patrick says Mattie is doing well on the medicine. Jean Marie is responsible. We're only going to be at the dress shop for a short time."

"I know," said Catherine, as she picked up her pocketbook and gloves. "I've been on pins and needles ever since Patrick warned me that Mattie could still suffer a heart attack if she overdoes. I may not even be going to the party."

She called to Mattie that they were leaving and went out the front door. The two young women descended the steps and took the brick walk out to the town sidewalk.

"Of course you are going to the garden party, even if you have to take Carrie Jo and Mary Margaret. I will help watch them," offered Carolyn.

"I want to have a relaxing time and so do you," said Catherine. "Keeping an eye on them is not my idea of relaxing."

"I've been giving a lot of thought to your situation. Have you thought of Grace Page, the milliner's sister? Charity said she was a good cook. Maybe she could take over some of Mattie's duties including helping with the children," suggested Carolyn. "You're going to need to find someone pretty soon."

They arrived at the corner of Church and Main Streets where Henry was sweeping the sidewalk in front of the Berryville Hotel. He doffed his cap and said, "Good mornin' ladies."

They stopped. "Good morning," they replied.

"You keep the hotel looking fine," said Catherine.

"Yes, ma'am. I ben' here ever since you owned the hat shop."

Henry was a little slow in the head, but he was always pleasant and a good worker.

"How's your baby, Miz' Carolyn?"

"She's growing up, Henry. She will start school in the fall."

Henry smiled. "That's good. I remember you had a bad time before the baby came."

"Yes," answered Carolyn and smiled. "All hunky-dory now."

Henry laughed. "Hunky-dory," he repeated. Henry may have been slow, but he had a good memory.

They waved to the barber on their way to the dress shop. The bell tinkled to announce a customer when they opened the door. Irene came from the back room. She had a turban around her head, mopping perspiration on her forehead and pushing her glasses back in place.

"Right on time," was her greeting. "Come on back here and try on your outfits. I hope they don't need altering. I'm pushed to the limit."

Carolyn smiled at her. "Think of all the compliments you're going to receive once the party's over."

"Compliments don't pay the bills," said Irene and turned to Catherine, "How's that new stove?"

"It works fine. I'm very pleased with it and so is my helper," answered Catherine.

"I heard Mattie had a heart attack," said Irene.

Catherine wasn't sure how the word got out, but it had and not accurately as most gossip seemed to be.

In a terse voice, Catherine set the story right. "No. Mattie did not have a heart attack. She's getting on in years and Dr. Burke said she could use some help."

Irene unwrapped the teal dress from a sheet she'd covered it with.

"Oh, my," said Catherine. "Mrs. Butler, it's lovely."

Irene gave a half smile. "Came out nice, I think. You go over in the dressing area and try it on. I made it to the exact measurements."

Catherine took her dress to the dressing area while Irene took Carolyn's outfit from its hanger. "I took in the skirt and the seams on the jacket. These manufactured clothes always need some finishing. You're going to look right smart."

Carolyn joined Catherine in the fitting area, and Irene came to lend a hand. "Are those the corsets you're going to wear?"

Both women looked puzzled as they nodded.

"I only ask that because some corsets are tighter than others. That makes a difference the way the dress fits. I should have told you before," Irene said.

"I remember from the last time you made a dress for me," said Carolyn,

Catherine laughed. "I don't know about you, but I only have one corset. They're expensive. I don't wear one around the house."

"Neither do I," said Carolyn. "Are you going to tell on us, Mrs. Butler?"

Irene looked up from inspecting the party outfits. "Corsets aren't usually a topic of conversation," she said, but she didn't say she wouldn't let the information slip.

A half hour later, Catherine and Carolyn were on their way back home, carrying their newly purchased garden party finery, and feeling happy about the whole experience.

Catherine looked over at Carolyn. "I think I'm going to make a visit to Grace Page. Will you bring Annie and stay at the house while I'm gone?"

Carolyn grinned. "A great idea. Do you want to go this afternoon? I can drop this package off at my house on the way. Annie's already over at your place, and my afternoon is free."

Before they turned the corner to go up Church Street, Catherine said, "I need a couple of things at Mr. White's general store. Do you mind if we stop by there?"

They made a short detour and went into the store. Catherine went around an end aisle and accidentally bumped into another customer while she reached for a can on the top shelf. "Oh, I am sorry. Please excuse me," she said.

The young lady turned to face her. "Miz' Catherine?"

"Oh, my goodness, Mary Lee! I haven't seen you in months."

Catherine smiled at the blue-eyed, red-haired, Mary Lee standing before her. Mary Lee's round face opened into a wide smile. "It sure has been a while," she replied. "I don't get into town much."

Mary Lee used to work for Catherine when she owned the hat shop. She was now married and lived on a big estate off of the Lord Fairfax Highway. Her husband was the farm manager.

"How are things with you, Mary Lee?"

"Not too good right now," she answered.

"Robert done hurt his foot, and he cain't work for a spell. That's why I come into town for some Epsom salts so's he can soak his foot."

"That's unfortunate," said Catherine.

Mary Lee was upbeat. "He'll be right fine in a few days."

It was then the thought hit Catherine that Mary Lee could use some extra money.

As Carolyn came around the corner to join them, Catherine said, "Mary Lee, I'm looking for someone to watch my two little girls on Saturday. Would you be available to help me out?"

Carolyn came to them. Mary Lee turned to greet her.

"Hello, Miz' Carolyn."

Carolyn held a surprised look. "Why Mary Lee, how nice to see you."

Catherine said to Carolyn, "I asked Mary Lee if she can watch the girls on Saturday."

That brought a big smile to Carolyn's attractive face. "That would be wonderful."

"I don't have an answer yet," said Catherine.

"Course I'll do it," interjected Mary Lee. "With Robert laid up, I can use some extra money, and beside it'll get me out of the house. Robert's like a bear when he can't get out on the farm."

That brought a big laugh from both Catherine and Carolyn. "I think that's the way with most men," said Carolyn.

"Would you like to stop by the house on your way home so you can meet the girls?" Catherine asked, "Or you could come by one day this week."

"I can come on Wednesday, if that's all right. I want to get these salts home so Robert can get busy soakin' that foot," Mary Lee replied.

"That will be perfect," said Catherine. "I believe it was fortuitous that we both ended up here at the general store."

Mary Lee laughed. "There you go usin's them big words, Miz' Catherine. I guess that means that's good."

"It couldn't be better," said Catherine. "I'll be home all day Wednesday, so whenever you can come will be fine."

Mary Lee took her goods to the counter while Catherine and Carolyn continued to search for what they needed.

After they left the store and started on their way up Church Street, Carolyn said, "That couldn't have worked out any better. I'm surprised you didn't think of Mary Lee sooner."

Catherine shook her head. "I know how busy she is taking care of her house and Robert, and she helps out on the farm. I would have thought it an imposition."

Carolyn laughed and looked over at her friend. "There you go, Miz' Catherine, usin' them big words."

Chapter 23

On Wednesday Mary Lee arrived at the Burke house, and so did Grace Page. Mattie was also present. As Mary Lee was going to watch the children on Saturday and Grace was considering helping in the house, Catherine wanted them to meet the children, familiarize them with the house, and most importantly meet each other.

Catherine, Mary Lee, Grace, and Mattie sat at the big dining table. Both Mary Lee and Grace appeared to be uncomfortable. Perhaps it was Mattie's dark suspicious eyes boring into them.

Catherine wasn't sure how to begin. The women sat so rigid that the room seemed to be closing in on her. She decided to conduct this the way she would a women's meeting. "Now that we've been introduced to each other, I thought it would be appropriate to talk to you ladies at the same time. Mattie, who has been my right hand helper for over five years has been ordered to take some time to rest. I have the three children and responsibilities within the community that I must fulfill, so I find myself in a quandary."

The women all looked at one another. Mattie shook her head, Grace seemed confused, and Mary Lee spoke up. "Miz' Catherine, maybe if you'd say it so we could understand, it would help."

Catherine gave a relieved laugh. "You're right Mary Lee. Sometimes I get carried away. First of all, I will need some help to watch the children. Mary Lee will be coming this Saturday to care for them while Dr. Burke and I attend a party, but there will be other times I will need someone. Grace, I need you to help with the laundry and cooking. I have a woman who works upstairs twice a week. She takes care of the linens and cleans the rooms up there. The rest of the laundry and ironing has been done by Mattie."

"How often do you need someone to watch the children?" asked Mary Lee. "With Robert laid up, I could help for a week."

Catherine smiled at her. "Thank you for offering. I need help when I have to attend meetings and volunteer at church. Usually they are scheduled ahead of time, but sometimes there is little warning."

"I can take care of my babies," said Mattie.

Catherine's attention went to Mattie. "Now you know that Mary Margaret still needs diaper changes and carrying at times. Those are the types of heavy lifting Patrick doesn't want you to do. Also, it's difficult to keep up with them when they go out to play."

Mattie rolled her eyes.

"Miz' Catherine," said Grace in her quiet voice. "I can help with the laundry and cooking if it isn't all day."

"What do you think, Mattie?" asked Catherine as a way of giving her maid some authority.

"Washin' clothes takes about three hours three times a week. I do it in the mornin'. I try to do the ironin' at the same time. There's always somethin' in the basket."

"Those are both jobs you can still help with," said Catherine.

"I suppose," answered Mattie.

"Grace, do you want to try it for a couple of weeks?" asked Catherine. "In the meantime, I will continue to look for other help."

Grace smiled. "That would be fine."

Catherine breathed an inner sigh of relief. She had Saturday and the two weeks following covered for now, and she could miss a meeting. The ladies would understand…or would they? At least she could relax at the garden party.

"It's time to go in and meet the children," she said. "All three are in the playroom with a young girl who lives down the street."

The noisy ruckus in the playroom stopped immediately when the four women appeared, and four pairs of eyes looked at them. Mary Margaret, shy of strangers, toddled over to her mother. "This is our baby," said Catherine as she picked her up and introduced her to Mary Lee.

"She's right sweet," said Mary Lee.

Catherine and Mary Lee walked over to the others. "This is Carrie Jo and John Patrick."

Jean Marie stood up from helping build blocks on the floor. "And, this is Jean Marie Moore. She lives down the street." To John Patrick and Jean Marie she said, "This is Mrs. Graves. She'll be taking care of the girls on Saturday."

Jean Marie smiled and said hello. John Patrick came to Mary Lee, held out his hand and said, "How do you do?" He was a perfect little gentleman and that pleased his mother.

Catherine went to Grace Page. "This is Miss Grace. She will be helping in the house."

Jean Marie and John Patrick repeated their greetings. Carrie Jo still looked unsure and edged closer to her mother.

Mary Lee hunched down so she was at eye level with Carrie. "You're a right pretty little girl with them blue eyes and blond curls. Do you like dolls?" Mary Lee reached into her handbag and brought out two cloth dolls she had made.

"They're adorable," Catherine said as she admired the handwork. "I see you still have the creative talent."

"So does Robert," said Mary Lee and brought a wooden car out of her bag for John Patrick.

"Holy cow," said John Patrick. "Isn't that a beaut, Mama?"

"You've been spending too much time around Mr. Asa," said Catherine.

All the women chuckled.

"I'm sorry I didn't know there was another pretty girl here," Mary Lee apologized to Jean Marie.

"That's all right," said Jean Marie. "I'm too old for dolls."

"But not for a bead bracelet," replied Mary Lee, and she reached into her bag and handed a string of colored beads on an elastic string to the young girl.

Jean Marie's eyes lit up, but she was tentative to accept it until Catherine said, "Go ahead. I'm sure your mother will allow it."

Jean Marie wasn't so sure as her mother was quite strict about anything she considered showy. The young girl slipped it over her wrist, and she smiled with pleasure. "Oh, thank you, Mrs. Graves. It's the prettiest thing I've ever had." Whether her mother approved or not, she was going to keep it. She could always hide it in her drawer. It seemed little Jeannie Moore was beginning to think like a teenager.

Chapter 24

At the Lockwood estate, Adelaide had finished her bookwork. It was noontime. Alex had gone into town, so Peg made a roast beef sandwich for her for lunch. Addie poured a glass of tea and sat on the back porch to eat. It was a day of huge fluffy clouds that usually meant a storm was brewing somewhere.

As she sat in the quiet, her mind turned to the garden party. Lottie was busy sewing her dress, and it was going to be lovely. It would feel grand to dress up again and leave the cares of the farm behind. The party will be a wonderful time, she thought.

Also, Jess had said that Fannie wrote. She was coming home on Thursday on the afternoon train. Jess told Addie that she could ride in with him to pick up Fannie if she wanted to. Addie had missed Fannie's presence from the farm as much as she had during the time Fannie and Jess went to California. But, that had worked out. Jess had gone to find his fortune. They hadn't become rich, but they were earning a good living from his investments. Soon they would be moving to a place of their own. Why do things always have to change?

Addie finished her lunch. It was time to go to see how her dress was coming along and lend a hand with the children. That had been her contribution, watching the children when Lottie needed to sew. It's good Fannie's coming back, thought Addie. She's much better with children than I am.

On the way down the path, the thought struck her that she should call Aunt Lilly at Roseville to ask if she'd be attending the Caldwell's party. It would make Addie more comfortable to know Aunt Lilly would be there. As it was, neither Lottie nor Fannie had been invited, and Clay and Rebecca Lockwood wouldn't be going. Rebecca was close to her due date for their second child. Addie smiled at the memory of Clay, the younger brother of Alex and so different. She knew Clay better than Alex did. While Alex had been sent away to boarding school, Clay and Addie grew up on the big family estate east of the town of Berryville. Clay was a Lockwood and both Addie and Lottie were daughters of hired help, but the three of them had a lot of fun together. Now Clay was expecting his second child and Alex had none, causing a fleeting pang of guilt for Addie.

She knocked on the screen door where she could see Lottie busy cleaning up the table where the children had eaten lunch.

"Come on in, Addie. I'll put the little one down for a nap and send Cal and Lizzie out to play."

"I saw the swing hanging from the tree. When did Caleb put that up?"

"Last Sunday after we got home from church. He also put in the sand bed. It keeps Cal and Lizzie busy and out from under my feet as long as they don't fight over who gets to swing," said Lottie. "I'm glad you're here. I need you to try on the dress so I can put in the hem."

Addie helped Lottie clean up the table while Lottie washed Cal and Lizzie's faces and hands before she shooed them out the door.

"Lottie, I don't know how you manage to do all you do. I shouldn't have let you get involved with making this dress. There are times when I can be selfish," admitted Adelaide.

Lottie smiled. "Are you just finding that out? Remember that I was the one who offered, so I can't blame anyone but myself."

She went to her bedroom and brought the dress into the living room. It was lavender lace over the pink silk.

"I'm excited about this," said Addie.

"You'd better be," said Lottie. "I knew when we bought the material it wouldn't be easy."

Addie slipped the dress on and stepped onto a stool so Lottie could measure the hemline. "I have a lovely pearl necklace that will go with the pearl buttons you've put on the cuffs."

"If you're going to wear your white straw, I think I have enough material to cover the crown. It would bring the whole outfit together," offered Lottie

"What a great idea. I can run up to the house and get it. By the way, Jess is going to the station to pick up Fannie tomorrow," said Addie.

"That must mean her mother's better. It'll be good to have her back. Caleb says Jess's mind is more on Fannie being gone than working on the farm," said Lottie.

Addie snickered. "It'll do him good to stew a little. I wonder what story will be in town once she returns?" said Addie.

Lottie shook her head. "Probably that she ran off with some man, and he left her flat. They can think up some good stories."

"Do you want me to pick up anything in town for you?" asked Addie.

"Can't think of anything," said Lottie.

Addie smiled to herself. She knew Lottie liked her sweets, so she would pick up a box of chocolates and a jar of hard candy for her friend.

When Addie got back to the big house, she asked Peg to take her hat to Lottie.

Addie went to the phone and called her aunt Lilly, who answered right away. "Aunt Lilly, this is Addie. Are you going to the Caldwell's garden party on Saturday?"

"Lilly knew that if her niece was excited about something, she got right to the point. "The answer is yes. We are planning on it, if nothing comes up in the meantime. Why do you ask?"

"Because Alex and I are going, and I'd feel more comfortable if knew someone there. When I go to these affairs, I feel like the odd man out."

"I'm sure there will be others you know. What about Clay and Rebecca?" asked Lilly.

"They're not going. Rebecca is close to her due date."

"That's wonderful," said Lilly. "I know she's hoping for a girl. How is she feeling?"

"I saw her about three weeks ago, and she was happy and doing well. I'm glad you were home to answer the phone, Aunt Lilly. As long as you're going, I feel better."

"Adelaide, you do have a tendency to over-think situations."

Addie laughed. "You know me well, Aunt Lilly. I'll see you on Saturday."

"Goodbye, Adelaide."

Addie hung up the phone and sighed. She thought about her sister-in-law. She knew Rebecca would be eagerly anticipating the arrival of a new baby, but Addie didn't feel up to sharing in her enthusiasm. No, not when she was sure Alex wanted an heir and she had yet to give him one. Then her mind switched to Fannie and she smiled to herself. Fannie's return was something she could get enthused about.

The next day, Addie rode into town with Jess. It was like a homecoming when Fannie stepped off the train. Jess hugged her and swung her around. He didn't care who saw him. Fannie laughed aloud. She came to Addie and hugged her. "Boy, I've missed this place," she said.

"We're happy you're back, Miss Fannie," said Addie in a playful mood. "You've had your hair cut. What happened to your pretty red curls?"

"They'll grow back," said Fannie. "I decided to try a new style."

"Are you hungry?" asked Addie.

"Starved," replied Fannie. "When Jess comes back with my bags, let's go to the Battletown."

They walked up Main Street to the inn. They were seated, and Harry West came to wait on them. "Mrs. Lockwood. It's nice to see you again. And, I see you have returned, Mrs. Edwards."

"Yes, I had to spend some time in Washington while my mother was ill."

Harry smiled. Never believe the rumors, he thought.

Jess walked in to join them. "Mr. Edwards," Harry said, "I was just telling your wife, it was good that she's back."

"I think we've all missed her," answered Jess.

They had their lunches of the daily special, left Harry a healthy tip, and stopped at the general store before climbing into the buggy to return to Lockwood. At the general store Addie bought Lottie's candy. It was a merry trip on the way back home, catching up on what had happened in Fannie's absence. When Addie mentioned the garden party, Fannie laughed.

"I'm looking forward to it," said Adelaide.

"You would," replied Fannie. "You love to get gussied up and hobnob with all those stiff people. I'm glad it's you and not me."

And in a quick moment all the concerns of Addie regarding the garden party came drifting back.

Chapter 25

On Thursday, Asa Thomas called Catherine on the telephone. "Catherine, I have a great crate here that would make a play fort for John Patrick. Are you interested?"

Catherine didn't need one more thing to complicate her day. She had the three children to care for and final touches to be ready for the Caldwell's party on Saturday. But Asa was a good friend, and it was thoughtful of him to offer. John Patrick was like the son he didn't have.

"I don't know, Asa. How big is it?"

"It's about six by eight. It would fit well in your back yard. He could play cowboys and indians."

"I'm sure he would love it. When will you bring it by?"

"I need to fix it up first. Not 'til sometime next week."

Catherine breathed a sigh of relief. "That's very kind of you, Asa. I won't tell him until you bring it, or he'll be asking me a dozen times 'when is it coming?'"

Asa laughed. "Carolyn said not to bother you today, but if you didn't want it, I was going to break it down. She said she can help with the children if you need her."

"That's good to know," replied Catherine. "Thank you, Asa."

"Guess we'll see you and Patrick tomorrow."

"That's the plan," said Catherine. "Goodbye and thanks again."

She'd fed the children breakfast and dressed them for the day. Patrick had ordered Mattie to stay home and rest. What was he thinking of? Today of all days she could use Mattie's help.

While the children were in the playroom, she had the breakfast dishes to wash and dry. Then she needed to get out the clothes that Patrick and John Patrick were going to wear to the party. They would need ironing, and she knew her white gloves could use a washing.

She was washing dishes at the sink when she heard a loud crash. Drying her hands on her apron as she ran to the playroom, her heart skipped a beat when she saw Carrie Jo laying on the floor and the bookcase toppled over. Mary Margaret was crying, and John Patrick stood stunned.

"Oh dear God," exclaimed Catherine. She hurried to her daughter.

"She was trying to climb up," said John Patrick, "and it just fell over."

By now, Carrie Jo had recovered and was crying along with her sister. Catherine picked them both up on her lap as she sat on a chair to collect herself.

Mary Margaret calmed down. Catherine set her on the floor, and she went back to exploring the toys. Carrie Jo stayed on her mother's lap. It was then Catherine noticed the swelling on Carrie's arm. Guilt crept in as she blamed herself for not looking the child all over before she swooped her up in her arms. Still not thinking straight, Catherine swaddled Carrie in her arms as she went to the telephone and called her friend.

"Carolyn get over here right away."

Carolyn, out of breath and with Annie in tow, was at Catherine's door as quickly as she could run up the street. There was no time to ring the bell as she barged right into the house. "What happened? You're white as a sheet!"

"I'm so glad you're here," said Catherine. "Johnny said Carrie was trying to climb up the bookcase, and it fell over. I think her arm is broken. I have tied a magazine around it to stabilize her arm."

"You sit down and take some deep breaths," Carolyn said to Catherine. Then she sat Carrie on the table and looked her over to see if there were any other injuries. "You'd better call Patrick. She has a little bruise on the side of her forehead and she may end up with a black eye, but she's going to need her arm taken care of."

Carolyn took Carrie in her arms while Catherine telephoned Patrick's office.

"He wants me to bring her right down," Catherine said to Carolyn. "Can you stay here?"

"Of course."

Catherine, in her everyday dress, put Carrie in the wicker carriage and rushed down Church

Street, headed for the Hawthorne House. Most likely every shop on Main Street had clerks and customers gawking out the windows, but Catherine paid no heed.

There was a waiting room full of patients, but Patrick came immediately and took Carrie right into the clinic room. He kissed her and said, "What's going on with my pretty little girl?"

Carrie Jo said, "Papa, my arm hurts."

"Well, we'd better fix that right up." He turned and put his arm around Catherine. "Are you all right?"

"Now that I'm here, I am. Carolyn is staying with the children."

Patrick smiled at her. "I must congratulate you on your improvised splint."

Catherine stared at him. How could he be so flippant? Of course he had seen far worse with all the maimed soldiers, but this is his child.

"Go sit in my office while I put a cast on her arm in the clinic room. I'll check her all over to be sure there aren't any hidden injuries," he said. "It's a clean break, so it should heal fine."

She let out an audible sigh. "That's a relief. I thought the bookcase was secure."

Patrick gave her a quick hug. "It's not your fault. Accidents happen. I'll have someone bring you a cup of tea."

Catherine's guilt wasn't soothed. "I know Mattie's going to have a fit and probably blame me. Or she'll blame you because you made her stay home today."

Patrick smiled. "She'll get over it. This could have happened while Mattie was there and given her a heart attack."

"Put it into perspective, love. It is a child's bookcase. It didn't fall on her, and she probably broke her arm when she fell and got that little bird's egg on the side of her head."

Catherine shook her head. "You do have an interesting way of looking at things." She kissed him on the cheek. "I'll be in your office."

It was thirty minutes later when Patrick carried Carrie Jo into his office. "I gave her a little something to ease the discomfort, but it'll wear off by the time you get home. Little ones bounce back quickly. Are you feeling better?"

"I've recovered," Catherine replied. "I left the carriage by the steps."

"If you're ready," Patrick said, "I'll carry her out."

The waiting room was crowded and all eyes were on the Burke family as they went down the hall to the front door.

"It looks like I'll be late getting home tonight," Patrick said as he put a groggy Carrie Jo in the carriage.

Catherine wrapped the blanket around her daughter. "I'm sure I'll be up as I have scads to do. I'd suggest you have dinner at the Battletown because there won't be anything but a sandwich at home."

"No four course dinner for your overworked husband?" he quipped.

"Dream on, Patrick. I'll see you at home if I survive this day." Then she kissed his cheek and wheeled the wicker carriage toward her large Victorian home on South Church Street.

When they got home, Carrie Jo was not too sleepy to show off her new plaster cast. "Papa fixed it," she said.

Carolyn had finished the dishes and had cleaned up the playroom. "One of the fixtures came out of the wall, Catherine. That's why the case fell over. I suspect Carrie has climbed on it before. You look a mess."

Catherine looked down and realized she still had her stained apron on over her housedress. She had gone without a hat and strands of hair were straggling down.

"Carolyn, why did you let me go looking like this?"

"As I recall," answered Carolyn, "we were a little distracted at the time."

Catherine laughed. "I don't want another scare like that. Why don't you and Annie stay for lunch?" invited Catherine. "I can make peanut butter and jam sandwiches."

"If it's Mattie's strawberry jam, I'm all for it."

It was a little after one o'clock when they finished their lunch of sandwiches, cookies, and tea. Carolyn was leaving, it was time for Mary Margaret's nap, and Carrie Jo was almost asleep, worn out from her morning's ordeal.

Catherine gave a heavy sigh. A relaxing day at the garden party was sounding better every minute.

Chapter 26

The unflappable and proper Harry West felt a twinge of excitement. The answer to his note said that she will be coming for the garden party and bringing a friend. They would arrive in Bluemont on the ten o'clock morning train on Saturday. That would be plenty of time for Harry to pick them up at the small Bluemont station, stop at his apartment to refresh themselves, and then travel the ten plus miles to the Red Gate estate.

Harry was in charge at the Battletown Inn, so he decided to close the inn on the Saturday of the party. He told the cook and the other waiter that most notable people in the area were the customers, and it was most likely they would be attending the big affair. After a moment of doubt whether or not the out of town owner of the inn would agree to close, Harry reminded them that he was in charge. All right, they said, as they had plenty of other things to do. Of course, that was after Harry told them they would receive their regular pay for the day.

It had been two years since he had seen Ella, except for the monthly letters. He had left Syracuse in a crestfallen mood after a romance that had gone sour. That's when he hopped into his Maxwell automobile, headed south on Route

11 and drove. He drove out of New York, straight through Pennsylvania, and stopped only for gas until he ended up in Winchester, Virginia. At that time, Harry wanted to get away and straighten out his thoughts. Wherever he landed was okay with him. He fully intended to return home when the hurt had left his soul. Then he saw the advertisement in the paper, and he was intrigued.

Harry knew the restaurant business. Waiting tables and pleasing customers was second nature to him. Harry left Winchester and went east, ten miles to Berryville and the Battletown Inn. He bought the inn in a private transaction with an out of town owner. This was Harry's secret, just as his previous life was kept to himself. To the Clarke County community, he was known as the waiter in charge of the Battletown.

A few days before the party, before Harry went to work, he went to the warehouse and worked on cleaning up the Maxwell. He wanted it to shine and be ready for his two guests. It would be cramped in the front seat meant for two not three. Who her friend was, Harry didn't know and hoped she would be on the slender side, allowing more room on the seat. Then he thought, perhaps the friend is not another woman. It made no difference.

Chapter 27

On Friday, Lavinia and Jeremy Talley came into the inn for lunch. Harry greeted them with a smile as he did all customers. "Good afternoon. It's always nice to see you," said Harry. "We have your favorite as a special today, Mrs. Talley."

Lavinia was all atwitter. "Did you prepare it especially for me?"

"You were on my mind," replied Harry, but he didn't say in what capacity. Lavinia was not one of his favorite customers. However, business was business.

Lavinia and Jeremy both settled for the special of cream of mushroom soup and a bacon, lettuce and tomato sandwich. "Did you hear that Dr. Burke's little girl broke her arm?" asked Lavinia.

Harry's smile faded. "No. How did it happen?"

"I was told that their maid is laid up, and Catherine was supposed to be taking care of the children. She was letting little Carrie Jo climb up a bookcase. The bookcase toppled over, and so did she. It was lucky she only ended up with a broken arm."

"I'm sure Mrs. Burke wasn't being neglectful," said Harry.

"Perhaps not," said Lavinia. "That's what I was told. And, I heard Dr. Burke was very upset about the whole incident. Anyone knows you don't allow a child to climb on a bookcase."

Harry let the matter drop. Lavinia was always ready to believe the worst.

As Jeremy and Lavinia were leaving, Carolyn and Asa Thomas came in.

Lavinia stopped her. "Carolyn, what is this I hear about Catherine's little girl breaking her arm?"

"It was an accident," replied Carolyn. "Patrick set it, and it's going to be fine."

"I just don't understand Catherine letting her climb around like that."

Carolyn gave a sweet smile. "Patrick needed some experience in casting a child's arm," she answered. "It's good to see you Mrs. Talley." With that, Carolyn and Asa followed Harry to their table.

Lavinia left in a huff.

Asa said confidentially, "Carolyn, I believe you have offended Mrs. Talley."

"Carolyn grimmaced. The woman gets on my nerves."

"Everyone's," whispered the staid Harry West. In his usual waiter's perfect diction, he said, "We have this table by the window. May I bring you a pot of tea?"

"Tea for my wife, and I'll have a good cup of coffee," answered Asa. "And, we decided on your vegetable soup and fried green tomatoes before we came. I have a busy day at the farm store."

"That's always good to hear," remarked Harry. "We had to scrimp during the wartime. I shall return post haste." That brought a chuckle from his customers.

When Harry returned with their food, Carolyn said, "I saw the sign that you will be closed tomorrow?"

"Yes," he said, "I will be going to the Caldwell's party."

"Are you bringing a friend?" asked Carolyn.

Asa frowned at her as it was none of her business.

"As a matter of fact, I'll be bringing too," Harry said.

Carolyn raised her eyebrows. Harry did not explain further.

"Then we shall hope to see you there," said Asa.

There was a finality in his tone that Carolyn knew she was not to say another word.

When they got to the street, Carolyn said, "I wonder who Harry is bringing to Elizabeth's party?"

Asa looked at her. "If he wanted you to know, he would have offered. If you're going by Catherine's, tell her I'll bring that play fort next Wednesday."

"I am stopping by. With Mattie out of the picture, Catherine can use some moral support."

Asa squeezed her hand. "I'll be home for supper." They went in opposite directions.

Inside the Battletown, Harry West was rather pleased with himself. By the time Saturday was over, the mystery man who had arrived in Berryville a little over two years ago, the brunt of many rumors, would no longer be a question mark.

Carolyn decided to stop and see Catherine as Annie still had an hour at the cotillion class. She was surprised to see Mattie answer her knock.

"Good afternoon, Mattie. I'm glad to see you up and around."

"Yes, ma'am," replied Mattie. "Miz' Catherine's back in the kitchen."

John Patrick came running from the playroom when he heard her voice. "Hi, Miss Carolyn. Is Annie with you?"

"Not today," said Carolyn.

"Applesauce!" exclaimed John Patrick.

Carolyn raised an eyebrow. "Applesauce?"

"Mr. Asa said when things don't go the way I want, that's a good word to say."

Carolyn had to smile. John Patrick put a lot of stock in what her husband taught him.

Catherine came from the direction of the kitchen carrying a striped man's shirt. "I heard voices," she said. "Mattie you are to sit in the playroom, not be up on your feet."

Mattie rolled her eyes. "Guess I'd better. I don't want my Carrie Jo breakin' another arm."

Catherine grimaced. "Come on out while I finish ironing Patrick's shirt," she said to Carolyn. "I let Mattie sit and watch the children as I was in a pinch to get our clothes ready for tomorrow."

"Can I help?" offered Carolyn.

"No thanks. I'm almost done. You can sit and talk to me while I finish up."

Carolyn followed her friend to the kitchen, and Mattie resumed her seat in the play room.

"I didn't want to bother Mattie, but I know she's getting restless. She gave me a time about Carrie's accident. The cast doesn't seem to slow my daughter down."

"She's always been curious," said Carolyn. "She likes to do her own thing, and that's good."

Catherine smiled. "Except when she turns over the bookcase," replied Catherine. "Do you want a cup of tea?"

"No thanks, I just came from the Battletown. Asa and I had lunch there. And, listen to this. Harry West is going to the garden party and bringing two guests."

Catherine gave a surprised look. "That's interesting. This party may turn out even more entertaining than I'd hoped for."

"I also saw Lavinia Talley. The word is that you let Carrie Jo climb the bookcase, and Patrick was livid."

Catherine set the iron down on the ironing board. "That sounds like her. Wait until she sees Harry West bring two guests. That may give her apoplexy."

Carolyn laughed. "You haven't got one of Mattie's oatmeal cookies around have you? I didn't have time for dessert at lunch."

Catherine finished ironing the shirt and hung it on a hanger. "How did you know? She's supposed to be resting at her house, and she came with cookies for the children. She always makes a bunch. Sure you don't want a cup of tea?"

"No, I'll eat it on my way to pick up Annie."

"How are her lessons going?" asked Catherine.

"I believe she will become the proper young lady, if I can get her to stop climbing trees."

Catherine laughed. "Be careful, if she falls and breaks her arm, they'll have you heading for jail."

Carolyn shook her head. "That's what I love about the town. Creativity is alive and well."

Chapter 28

In Washington, D.C., Ella West Fleming was happy. A day in the country would be a welcome change from the day to day grind in the city. She wondered why her brother, Harry, had decided to invite her. It had been two years since she had seen him in person, even though they lived only seventy miles apart. Of course there had been the monthly check and a small note, but it didn't reveal much about his present life. Ella sighed. Running the restaurant must be what takes up his time, she thought.

Ella was a few years younger than Harry, which put her in her late twenties. She was too young to be a widow, but she was and had been for almost three years. That was a bad year when Art died, not only for her, but also for Harry, who was beginning to see his dreams fade as the woman he hoped to marry became cooler and cooler to his entreaties.

In fact, thought Ella, it was shortly after Arthur's unexpected death that Harry seemed to have vanished into thin air. About a month later, she did receive a telegram that said he was alive and well.

Arthur Fleming, Ella's dead husband, owned an investment firm. He decided to move to Washington where he would be close to the political scene and to men with money who wanted to invest. If he got the inside scoop of what was to be big business, that would be all the better for Fleming Investments, Inc.

Arthur was close to forty when Ella married him. She was twenty-one and a graduate of a business school for women. She became his secretary and learned his business from the ground up. They were only in Washington for a year when Art died. Ella was left with Fleming Investments, Inc. and a dwindling supply of customers. Men did not believe in a woman running a business.

Ella was smart, and she had to survive. She rented out three rooms in her big house to cover everyday costs. Arthur had bought the stately home because he said it would make him look prosperous. Anything that was good for business was fine with Arthur Fleming. Many of her renters were those who had come to Washington for positions in the government and needed a room until they could find a permanent place. This arrangement worked well because the rooms were always occupied with paying customers.

Ella hired a woman to clean the rooms and offered no boarding lest the renters would get too comfortable. It also cut down on the expenses.

Then there was the business to run. Fleming Investments, Inc. remained the name because it didn't reveal there was a woman behind it. Nothing had to be changed except to remove Arthur's name wherever it appeared.

To keep the business afloat, she decided to make the rounds of widows. They were most likely to accept her, and they were women who needed to make what money they had work for them. Ella felt it was not only her Christian duty to help them, she also could keep the investment firm going. She was right. Word got around that Fleming Investments was a solid business. She began to get well-to-do wives and men with means who had no aversion to a woman running a business as long as it was profitable for them.

It didn't hurt that Ella was attractive and dressed in the up-to-date styles. Her personality was much like Harry's, so were her blond hair and blue eyes. Ella West Fleming had a way of making people feel comfortable.

The friend she was bringing to the garden party was a younger girl with the name of Claire Murphy. She was a rather quiet young lady of average height who reminded Ella of Snow White. Claire seemed lost when she inquired about renting a room. Ella remembered herself feeling the same way when she moved to Washington, but she had Arthur. Claire had no one. Ella took it upon herself to be the younger girl's mentor. She found a spot in her business for Claire and insisted she take some courses to gain some office skills. If Claire didn't want to stay in the investment business, Ella felt she would acquire the knowledge to work in any office.

At this time, Claire was still renting a room and working for Ella. She had agreed to attend the party so Ella didn't have to travel on the train by herself. Besides, Claire Murphy liked the peacefulness of the country. Also, she wanted to meet Ella's brother. Claire wanted to see the expression on Ella's face when she and her brother were together again. Ella was a good friend who had led her out of her cloistered view of the world. Yes, thought Claire, it would be an interesting day.

Chapter 29

A couple of hours before the evening meal, Grace Page arrived at Catherine's house in the late afternoon on Friday. If she was expected to use that newfangled stove at the Burke house, she wanted to be prepared. And, if she was going to start working on Monday, she needed to get the feel of where she would be working. It was a relief to know there was a woman who took care of the upstairs. This was all new to Grace as she had never worked outside of her home. Her mother was well enough to watch the children, and they were getting to the age where they didn't need much watching.

Saying a quick inner prayer, Grace raised her hand to knock on the front door of the stately Victorian house. She wondered if she should have gone to the back of the house instead. Catherine answered her knock.

"Grace, I'm so pleased to see you. This has been a very busy day. Come out to the kitchen. Mattie is here to show you around. How is everything at your house?" Catherine asked.

Grace nodded, "Jus' fine, thank you."

Mattie was sitting at the kitchen table peeling potatoes. She raised her eyes when they came into the room. "You ladies have met," said Catherine, "so if you need me, I'll be in the sewing room or with the children."

Mattie gave her a questioning look.

"I'll have Mary Margaret with me Mattie. John Patrick and Carrie Jo play well together."

"I sure was sorry to hear about your little girl breakin' her arm," said Grace. "Is it goin' to heal all right?"

Catherine smiled at her. "Thank you for asking. Dr. Burke says it will be fine in a few weeks."

Grace smiled back. "That's good to hear."

Catherine went on her way, and Mattie remained in her seat. She nodded to Grace to sit across from her. The woman could be intimidating.

Grace quietly took the chair across from Mattie and folded her nervous hands in her lap. She waited for Mattie to break the silence.

Mattie began after a tense moment. "It is good you're here. Mistah' Patrick has ordered me to slow down, and I can't do what I used to do, at least right now I can't, so he sez'."

Grace relaxed a bit. "He's a good doctor."

Mattie almost smiled. "I ben' takin' care of him since he was little."

"That's a long time," replied Grace. "You probably know him better than his own momma."

These words pleased Mattie, and the ice was broken. "Probly' so," she said. "I'm peelin' these potatoes to make a salad. Soon's I finish, I'll show you where things are at an' what's needed." Then she laughed. "An' don't let that contraption over there scare you. It's like to put me under when I saw the fancy stuff on it."

Grace gave a wary eye toward the stove. "It sure is pretty,"

"It works good. Course you have to get used to it, not like cookin' on a good wood stove."

"You'll have to teach me, Miz' Mattie." Grace went up a couple notches on Mattie's acceptance list. "Can I help you put the salad together?"

Mattie pointed to a drawer that held another paring knife and pushed an onion, radish, and dill pickle toward Grace. "You can cut these up. I always like to put them in my potato salad. I like cucumbers, too, but it's too early for them."

Grace washed her hands at the sink, found the knife, and sat at the table. Maybe this won't be so bad after all, she thought.

By the time they finished putting the salad together, they were chatting like old friends. Mattie showed her the wash room with the tubs, washboard, and soap. "I use the *Arm&Hammer* for regular clothes and the *Fels-Naptha* for the real hard stuff. Kids can get plenty dirty." Then Mattie laughed. "Here I am tellin' you an' you got four of your own."

Grace offered a quiet smile.

"There's plenty of room on the clothesline out back. I do the washin' on Monday and Thursday. The woman who takes care of the upstairs does the linens on Tuesday and Friday. Friday's ironing day so everything's ready for church and company."

They went back into the kitchen. "I keep that bottle of lanolin up on the window ledge for my hands. You're welcome to use it so they don't get chafed."

"Where do you find the dirty clothes?" Grace asked.

"Mostly, Miz' Catherine brings them to me. I pretty much pile the tablecloths, towels, and dishcloths over in that barrel in the laundry room." Mattie shook her head. "Should have told you."

It was time to tackle the *Peerless* stove. Mattie was in her prime and was about to give Grace her first lesson of cooking on an electric stove. By the time they were finished, Grace held a puzzled look. "I guess if you stand right there with me, I might be able to figure it out," she said in a tentative voice.

"Course you will," encouraged Mattie. "I think we 'bout covered everything Miz' Catherine wants you to do. Sometimes we butt heads 'cause she's just as stubborn as I am."

Grace Page said in her shy way, "I hope this will work out. I thank you, Miz' Mattie. I ben' frettin' over this since I said I'd try it. You helped get rid of the jitters."

Mattie felt better, also. She liked Grace, a woman who wasn't going to take Mattie's rightful place in the Burke household. Although she didn't want to admit it, Mattie knew she had to slow down. But that didn't mean she couldn't sing to her babies or give them extra love, especially Johnny who was so like his father.

Chapter 30

It was early Saturday morning when the phone rang. Patrick answered it with a sleepy voice. "How far apart?" he said.

Catherine awoke and heard those words. She'd heard them before and knew it had to be a woman in labor. Her heart sank. Today will be the garden party that she had prepared for so carefully. Perhaps Thaddeus Hawthorne could stand in for Patrick.

He hung up the phone and continued sitting on the edge of the bed. "That was Clay Lockwood," he said as he pulled on his socks. "Rebecca's baby is on the way."

Catherine turned to her side. "Can't Thaddeus take over for you?"

"I wish he could, but he has to go up to the Winchester hospital to check on two patients we have up there. He's taking Grace with him, and they'll travel down to Red Gate from there."

Catherine sat up with a pout on her face. "That isn't fair. I've looked forward to this party for weeks."

Patrick was putting on his shirt. "I know, and I'm sorry. With any luck she'll deliver in a few hours. We can still make Red Gate. If I can't get back, you can ride down with Asa and Carolyn."

He buckled his belt and put on his jacket before he leaned down and kissed her forehead. "Don't let this disappointment ruin your day. It will all turn out."

Catherine gave a weak smile. "You always say that, and it usually does. I'll call Carolyn when I get up. Go deliver your baby. As for me, it's only five o'clock which means I've got a couple more hours of sleep." She laid back on the bed and pulled the covers over her head.

By eight-thirty, Catherine had eaten and fed the children oatmeal for breakfast. She was washing Mary Margaret's hand and face when Mattie came in the back door. She looked around the kitchen with an expression that said "this woman makes a mess," but she only rolled her eyes. "What time are you goin'?" she asked.

"It starts at one o'clock," said Catherine. "Patrick is out on a house call, and I don't know when he'll be back. I have to call Carolyn to see if John Patrick and I can ride with them."

Mattie started to clean up the soiled dishes on the table.

"Just put them on the sink board. I'll wash them after I call Carolyn."

Mattie shook her head. "No reason I can't do dishes."

Catherine kissed her youngest and set Mary Margaret on the floor. She toddled off to find the toy room. "I guess not," Catherine said to Mattie. "I'll dry them and put them away."

Mattie didn't protest as it would keep Miz' Catherine's mind busy before it was time to get ready for that uppity party she was so bent on going to.

"Good morning, Carolyn," Catherine greeted her over the phone. "I hope I'm not disturbing you."

"Hello, Catherine," replied Carolyn. "I'm finishing a late breakfast." She waited for Catherine to give her reason for calling.

"Patrick is on a house call, and I'm not sure when he will return. I need to ask if John Patrick and I can ride to Red Gate if he isn't back in time."

"Well, surely you are welcome to ride with us. Did Patrick think he wouldn't be back?"

Catherine couldn't tell Carolyn over the phone that Rebecca Lockwood was in labor or the word would be all over Berryville. Perhaps the news was already spreading from Clay's call. It all depended on who the night telephone operator was. "He wasn't sure. Dr. Hawthorne can't cover for him because he has to see patients in the Winchester hospital."

"That's too bad. Asa said we need to leave a bit after noon. We will stop and pick you up. Annie will be happy to have John Patrick along," Carolyn said.

"We'll be ready and waiting on the porch. Thank you, Carolyn. I knew I could count on you."

Carolyn laughed. "Elizabeth would never forgive me if you didn't show up. The three of us together again since Christmas. The days seem to travel too fast."

Catherine chuckled. "That's true. It seems I fall into bed and it's time to get up."

"I can't wait to see you in your new outfit," said Carolyn.

"And you in yours. Elizabeth will be pleased. I'll see you around noontime. Goodbye Carolyn."

"Bye Catherine."

Catherine hung up the earpiece on the hanger and went to help Mattie in the kitchen. She felt relieved. If Patrick didn't make it back, she was going to the big affair anyway. As Patrick had said, it would all work out.

Mary Lee Graves arrived at ten o'clock to care for Carrie Jo and Mary Margaret. She brought a tote bag with her with hand-made puppets and handwork to keep her busy when the girls napped.

Mattie went home at Catherine's request after they had cleaned up the kitchen. "You've done enough this morning, Mattie. Mary Lee will watch the girls while I get ready to go. I told her if she needs anything she can go and ask you."

That made Mattie feel important, and she didn't mind a bit about having to take an afternoon of rest.

Chapter 31

Adelaide Lockwood was up early after a restless night's sleep. Today was the big party, and Fannie and Lottie would be coming for coffee around nine o'clock. Lottie had not seen Fannie since she had returned from caring for her mother in Washington. Lottie also wanted to take a final check of Adelaide's dress to be sure there were no minor repairs as Addie always wanted to look her best.

Alex was in the office. He looked up and smiled when Addie came into the room. The once indoor lawyer was beginning to show the effects of outdoor farming.

"What time are we leaving?" asked Addie.

"Noon would give us an hour. Did you say Fannie and Lottie were coming for coffee?"

Addie nodded. "Yes, They'll be here in a few minutes."

Alex put some papers in a folder. "I need to go out and talk with Caleb and Jess."

Addie wrinkled her nose. "Be sure and keep an eye on the time. I know how it is when you three get talking. I don't want to be late."

"Promise," he replied. "You were restless last night. Feeling alright?"

She offered a weak smile. "I guess I was a bit wound up about today."

He glanced out the window. "Looks like we've got a pretty day for it."

"Yes we do." said Addie as she was turning to leave. "Remember. We are to leave at noon."

Alex just smiled.

When Fannie and Lottie arrived, Addie decided to sit on the wide front porch to have their coffee. "Where are your children?" she asked Lottie.

"Caleb, Jess, and Alex are having coffee in my kitchen while I'm up here. Caleb says it's easier to solve problems over a cup of coffee. The kids are home with them."

The three young women went to the porch. They were a cohesive trio: level-headed, down-to-earth Lottie; matter-of-fact with a touch of cynicism Fannie; assertive, and a tinge of bossiness Adelaide.

They sat at a wicker table. "The Blue Ridge is hazy today," remarked Fannie as she looked off in the distance. "Probably going to be warm."

"It should be nice under those big oak trees," said Lottie. "It sure is a pretty spot down at Red Gate. I haven't been in that end of the county in a long time."

Addie showed a bright smile. "I'm looking forward to it."

"You would," said Fannie. "You like to get all spiffed up and hob-nob with the landed gentry."

Addie huffed and grimaced at her. "That's not true. Why are you so sour this morning?"

"Jess wants to go looking for our own place."

"What's the matter with that?" Lottie asked.

"I like it here in that little cabin with the stream behind it. I've planted a nice flower and vegetable garden. Besides, I don't want to move too far from here"

"What makes you think he wouldn't settle close?" Addie said.

Fannie looked over at her, "You know Jess. He's like you. He's got that itchy foot and always wants to see what lies over the hill. He wants his own place."

Addie chuckled. "I admire his adventuresome spirit."

Fannie shrugged her shoulder. "I guess you call it that."

"Maybe he should wait 'til something near is up for sale or somebody wants to sell off part of their farm. Caleb says he heard that old Harvey Smith is getting strapped for cash," Lottie informed.

Addie let out a disgusted snort. "I wonder who spread that word? He's a nice man, and people shouldn't gossip like that."

Fannie shrugged. "It's probably true."

Addie looked at her. "I don't care. People's private business should be their private business."

Fannie laughed. "Around here?"

"I brought cookies to have with our coffee," injected Lottie as a way of changing the subject.

"Yummy," remarked Fannie. "What kind?"

"Kind of a mixture. There's peanut butter, sour cream with strawberry jam, molasses, and an experiment. I had some leftover applesauce and mixed it in with the oatmeal. They're kind of soggy, but I think they taste good."

Peg came out to the porch with their coffee. "I brought the china pot, that way your coffee will stay warm." She put the pot, sugar and cream in the middle of the table before she set out the cups and saucers.

Lottie removed the lid from her tin container and set it on the table. Peg looked at the cookies then at Lottie. "You should open a bakery."

Lottie laughed. "I couldn't. I'd eat all the profit."

Peg put a spoon in each cup before she poured the coffee to absorb some of the heat and not crack the fine china cups.

Lottie passed the tin of cookies. "Peg, take some cookies before you go back in the house."

"Just leave me a couple on your way out," Peg replied and left the women to enjoy their morning.

"I want to make a final check of your dress, Addie. Do you think it's all right?" Lottie asked.

"It looks fine to me," Addie answered.

"I haven't even seen it," Fannie piped in. "I'm ready for the unveiling."

They all chuckled.

"Once we're done with our coffee," said Addie.

They ate and laughed and finished their coffee. It was ten-thirty when Addie brought out her dress of lavender lace over a pink underlining.

Fannie took in a breath. "Lottie, you outdid yourself. It's beautiful."

"It's one of the prettiest I've ever had, except maybe for that taffeta one you made for me in Colorado. Do you remember that one, Lottie?"

Lottie made a face. "How could I forget? It was a bugger to put together."

Fannie shook her head. "I wish I could have been on that trip."

Lottie smiled. "I only went because Addie wanted to go. We were eighteen and silly teenagers. I'm perfectly happy to be settled here."

A mild admonishment came from Addie. "Don't forget that you met Caleb in Colorado. And, we weren't silly teenagers. It was an enlightening trip."

"I still wish I'd been with you," Fannie said.

Addie looked at her and smiled. "You would have found some hard-headed cowboy and settled down out there."

Fannie nodded. "You're probably right. Instead, I found one right here, thanks to you."

"What are friends for?" was Addie's witty reply.

Chapter 32

Catherine and John Patrick were waiting on the porch when Asa drove up the circle drive in his red Model T Ford. Red was a bold color for the conservative Asa Thomas. Carolyn and Annie were sitting in the front seat. Asa opened the door of the car and stepped out as Catherine and John Patrick were coming down the stairs. Asa maintained his athletic build, although there was bit of widening around his middle.

John Patrick ran to him. "Hi, Mr. Asa. We've been waiting for you."

Asa picked him up and whirled him around. "You have, have you? You look mighty dapper in those knickers."

John Patrick laughed. "I guess that means I look good. Mama said I'm not to get dirty before we get to the party."

"Go hop in the back seat." He went to meet Catherine as she descended the steps. Asa offered his arm as they walked to the car. "You look lovely," he remarked.

Catherine slipped her hand around his elbow. "Thank you for picking us up. We may have to ride home with you if Patrick doesn't make it to Red Gate."

"That's no problem, but I think he will be missing a nice afternoon."

He opened the back door of the sedan. Catherine stepped up on the running board and settled into the back seat before Asa closed the door and took his place in the driver's seat.

Turning her head toward the back seat, Carolyn greeted her. "Hi, Catherine, your teal outfit almost shines in the sun."

"I hope not," said Catherine. "I don't want to look like a hussy."

Carolyn laughed. "You will never pass for a painted lady. Have you heard from Patrick?"

"No. I assume Rebecca's baby hasn't made it into this world yet."

"I can hardly wait to see Elizabeth."

Asa chuckled as Church Street turned into the Lord Fairfax Highway. "I can honestly say that I'm glad the day has arrived so my dear wife can unwind."

Carolyn looked over at him. "Asa thinks I've been over-preparing."

Catherine sighed. "This past week has been one I don't wish to do again."

Carolyn nodded. "I know. Me either. Did Mary Lee get there on time?"

"You know dependable Mary Lee. I was happy to see her. Mattie actually said she was going to rest this afternoon. I do worry about her," admitted Catherine.

Carolyn turned her head to look at Catherine. "As long as she follows Patrick's instructions, she should do all right. She is trying isn't she?"

"She's trying for sure," quipped Catherine, and they both laughed.

At Old Chapel, a train was going across the overpass. "Papa, can we stop and watch it?" said Annie, who had been quiet up to this point. "I like to count the cars."

John Patrick sat up straight to look through the front windshield. "Me too," he said.

So, Asa pulled the car to the side of the road while Annie and John Patrick silently counted the cars. When the caboose came in sight all windows were rolled down in the auto, and they waved their hands at the flag man on the back. He gave a hearty wave back as the train rambled off down the track.

They wound their way through the hamlet of Millwood, past Locke's store and the Burwell-Morgan mill.

Carolyn said, "I remember coming through here when James Anderson drove me from the Winchester hospital so I could care for Virginia Caldwell. I was a new graduate nurse."

"Did you enjoy it?" asked Catherine.

She offered a pensive sigh. "It was an interesting time. I guess I can say I enjoyed it. I think it was a time of growing up."

Asa looked over at Carolyn and smiled. "That's where we met," said Asa. "I agree with Carolyn that it was an interesting time."

Catherine smiled to herself. Carolyn had told her about the times she had spent at Red Gate and there had been some strained moments between James and Asa. Both vied for her attention.

It was fifteen minutes before one o'clock when they arrived at the estate. A man stood at the open red iron gates and directed Asa to the place cars were to be parked. Before parking, Asa stopped at the brick walk that led to the back of the big house where his four passengers departed the automobile.

"Can you believe we're finally here?" said an enthused Carolyn.

"I'm glad," replied Catherine. "It should be an eventful day with all the preparation Elizabeth says has gone into it."

"I guess we'll find out," answered Carolyn. Let's go find our hostess."

Chapter 33

The pretty blonde, blue-eyed Elizabeth, in a soft silk robin's egg blue outfit, held a wide smile as she came to meet her friends, admiring their stylish attire as she came to them. "What a vision of loveliness," she remarked and hugged them both.

"You're only saying that because it's true," replied Carolyn, bringing a chuckle from the two lady friends.

"I'm quite sure I see Irene Butler's hand in your outfits, but where did you get the lovely hats?"

Catherine smiled. "In Josephine city. Grace Jackson knows her millinery."

"I will have to keep that in mind," said Elizabeth.

Annie and John Patrick had been quiet minding their polite manners.

Elizabeth hugged them both. "Look at you two. Annie with a beautiful dress and hair bow to match, and John Patrick with his sharp looking jacket and knickers. Matthew has been asking all morning when you were going to get here."

At that moment Asa walked to them on the brick walk after parking the car.

"Asa how good to see you. Where is Patrick?" Elizabeth asked. "I thought he would be with you."

Catherine offered a wan smile. "He's delivering Rebecca Lockwood's baby."

"How exciting!" Elizabeth exclaimed. "We will miss him."

Replied Asa,"We're hoping he can still make it. It seems babies have their own sense of timing."

"That's true," Elizabeth agreed. "Come and I'll show you what we've set up before any other guests arrive."

They walked to where the white tables and chairs were set up behind the red brick manor house. The yard was wide and spacious. Food and drink tables were set under the tall oak trees. A pond lay in an area down the slope of the lawn, a path led to the stables, far enough away to keep the smell of livestock away from the house. It was a beautiful view of the vast estate holdings and the Blue Ridge Mountains sitting quietly in the distance. The day was warm with a slight breeze.

"Matthew is down by the stables with his father." Elizabeth said to the children. "He's been asking all morning when you were coming."

"Can I go, Mama?" asked an antsy John Patrick.

"May I go," corrected Catherine. "Yes, you may. Stay away from the pond or you'll get wet and muddy."

Annie looked at her mother and Carolyn gave a permissive wave of her hand. That's all it took for the two to race off to find Matthew.

"I'll keep an eye on them," said Asa. "I'm going to the stables to see Andrew. I won't promise the kids will stay clean."

Elizabeth offered a warm smile. "Thank you, Asa. Andrew will be glad you're here. There's a new foal he's excited about."

The guests were beginning to arrive, so Catherine and Carolyn gravitated to the flower garden behind a row of boxwoods where Emily Caldwell was plucking an errant weed.

"Emily," called Carolyn as she spied her bending down.

Emily straightened up and turned. "Oh, Carolyn. My goodness, it's so good to see you. Elizabeth said you would be coming. You could pass for a model in that outfit. It's absolutely gorgeous."

Carolyn laughed as she gave Emily a quick hug.

The demure Emily grinned. "You're still one to lift my spirits," she said, bringing back the memories of how Carolyn had helped her to climb out of the world of alcohol.

"You remember Catherine, don't you?" asked Carolyn as Catherine came to where they stood.

"Yes, of course. How are you Mrs. Burke? Elizabeth has told me you and Dr. Burke have three children."

Catherine nodded. "We do. They keep me busy."

"It's so good of you to come." Emily offered a sincere smile. "Elizabeth wants me to check to see if the musicians need anything. That was after she asked me to take one last tour of the garden, which I find in good shape. So, please excuse me while I go off to check on the merrymakers."

There was a commotion in Elizabeth's direction. Lavinia Talley had arrived with Jeremy and a photographer. From where they stood they could see Lavinia was all afluster.

The two women looked in the direction of the bandstand and noticed it was close to the old hop kiln where Elizabeth and Emily had set up a school for the farm children.

"Catherine, let's go over to the hop kiln before Lavinia spots us. You've never seen how Elizabeth and Emily fixed that up," said an adventurous Carolyn.

"You had better ask Elizabeth. I don't want to look like a busybody," replied Catherine.

"Come on, the door's ajar, I can see it from here. Elizabeth won't mind. Besides, she's busy being the hostess."

"Ask Emily. She's right near there. I'm not going to go without someone saying it's allowed."

"Good heavens," said Carolyn. "There are times when you can be a stick-in-the-mud."

"Rather a stick-in-the-mud than a trespasser," answered Catherine. Carolyn shook her head. "We'll go ask Emily,"

"Certainly, go right in," was Emily's response. "We call it our first aid station for the party, in case there's a scraped knee or someone feels faint."

"That is forward thinking," said Catherine.

Emily chuckled. "I don't think Elizabeth missed one thing."

Catherine and Carolyn stepped into the ten by twelve room. The eight desks had been pushed to one side to make room for a cot. On the teacher's desk were a first aid kit, towels, washcloths, soap, and a bowl for water. There was a pump and pail outside for well water.

The blackboard was on the back wall. Carolyn wrote her name and then erased it. "Do you remember how we had to help wash and clean the slate?" she said.

Catherine nodded. "I hated cleaning out the erasers. All that chalk flew around. I used to go home and wash my hair after it was my turn to help the teacher."

"I'll bet you were a teacher's pet," Carolyn said. "You probably always did your homework and handed it in neat and tidy."

"Certainly I did. That's what you're supposed to do in school," Catherine replied. "Didn't you?"

"I waited until the last minute, then hurried to get it done so I wouldn't get a zero. I didn't become a good student until I went to nursing school. I guess I grew up."

Catherine sighed, "We all have to. I say we go out and see who has arrived."

They could hear Lavinia ordering the photographer, Jimmy, around. Lavinia was waving her hands toward the musicians' platform. "One good thing," said Carolyn, "we haven't had to put up with Lavinia. I'm glad she brought Jimmy, but I'll bet he'll be careful about signing up again."

"He is beginning to look a bit harried, and they've just started," Catherine observed.

Through the open door they could see Lavinia's husband, Jeremy. He paid no heed to Lavinia and the photographer. He had notebook and pencil in hand and was scouting the periphery. After all, he was the editor of the *Clarke Courier.*

Catherine and Carolyn went to meet others. Mr. and Mrs. Moore with Jean Marie had arrived. Mr. Moore was an important businessman. His first wife died and he remarried. Jean Marie was a toddler, so Stella Moore was the only mother she knew. Stella, a staunch church-going woman, was cordial enough, but remained aloof. It was no wonder Jean Marie liked to visit the lively Burke house, thought Catherine.

Also present were the president and vice president of the Bank of Clarke County along with their wives. Rumor had it that there was a rift between the two couples. If there was, it wasn't noticeable as they looked quite compatible and had arrived together. Bankers couldn't afford a scandal.

"Look who just arrived," Catherine said without pointing. Dr. Hawthorne and Grace had made it down from Winchester. By then it was almost two o'clock, and there was no sign of Patrick. "I wish Thad had been the one to deliver Rebecca's baby."

"I hope everything is going well with that delivery," said Carolyn.

The three musicians had warmed up and were playing some classical pieces mixed in with old folk songs, with a Sousa march now and then to liven things up. By three o'clock the sandwiches of egg salad, chicken, ham, roast beef, and cucumber were being replenished along with the various salads of potato, cabbage, and vegetables. There were pickled beets, pickled cucumbers, and pickled eggs. All varieties of cheese were attractively arranged on plates. Dishes of peanuts and sugared walnuts were plentiful. There was a selection of cookies and dainty cakes on the dessert table. Ollie kept her kitchen crew busy, and they were quick to replace the foods along with the tea and lemonade.

Adelaide Lockwood arrived looking stunning in her lavender lace. She wanted to make a grand entrance and look the part of a suitable lady of the manor. Guests turned to take a second look and an audible catching of breath could be heard as she tripped over a stone. Alex caught her before she crumbled to the ground. Not only was it embarrassing, it caught the attention of those she most wanted to impress.

Adelaide's faux pas was quickly forgotten when Harry West arrived escorting two attractive ladies. He was the same Harry West known as the waiter at the Battletown Inn. Undertone murmurs went through the crowd. What was a waiter doing here?

Undaunted that he had caused a sensation, the impeccable Harry West escorted his two guests to the party where Elizabeth greeted them with a welcoming smile. "Miss Elizabeth, I'd like to have you meet my sister, Ella Fleming and her friend, Claire Murphy."

"I am delighted you could come," said Elizabeth. When she looked into the eyes of Claire Murphy, she felt she had met her before. There was no recognition from the reserved Claire. "There's plenty of food, and I know Harry can introduce you to many people here."

"I apologize for being late, but their train wasn't on time," Harry told Elizabeth.

"There is no need for an apology," said Elizabeth "A group is coming up from the stables so you might want to head for the food table before they get here."

"We heard the music. It lends a pleasant mood," Ella commented.

Elizabeth chuckled. "They're a baroque group. Once in a while they play a Sousa march to wake everyone up."

Harry and his two guests went to join the party, and Elizabeth went to mingle and keep an eye on the big affair. The garden party was going well.

A few minutes later, Patrick arrived. He found Catherine and Carolyn having food at a small table. "The Lockwoods have a beautiful baby girl. Made me wish we still had one in the cradle."

"Perish the thought," said Catherine. "How are Rebecca and the new one?"

Patrick winked at her. "Both mother and baby are doing well. I don't know about Clay, but

I think he's recovered. You'd think he was one in labor."

"You must be tired," said Catherine. I'll get you a glass of tea while you fill a plate."

"I'm tired and starved," admitted Patrick.

Carolyn rose from her seat. "I'm going to take a look at the pond," she said.

The women went their separate ways.

The horsey set were making their way back from the stables and heading for the food table. Among them was the handsome James Anderson. He noticed Carolyn walking toward the pond. James was not one to let an opportunity pass, so he picked up a couple of sandwiches from the food table and started in her direction.

Carolyn found a comfortable spot to sit on the ground and looked at the water. It wasn't deep but deep enough that Hannah had almost drowned her in it. The frightening feeling of her head being pushed up and down in that murky water gave her chills. It was Asa who had rescued her from the mad woman.

"Hello, Carolyn," came a deep voice behind her. She turned to look.

"James! You broke my reverie. Why aren't you back there talking horse talk?"

He laughed and lowered himself to sit beside her. "Because I'd much rather talk with my only love. By the way, you look fetching."

Carolyn smiled at him. "I'm sitting on my handkerchief hoping I don't get grass stains. You're quite daring sitting here. We'll likely be the next snip of gossip."

There's no one around. They're all en-grossed in themselves. Besides, aren't you glad to see me?"

Carolyn had to smile. "I'm always glad to see you. I can't say Asa would agree. He probably won't be pleased to see us sitting together away from the others. Where's your wife?"

"Off to England where she says she has her true family, which means an old dowager who sends her a letter once a year." There was disgust to his tone.

"You shouldn't have married her." Carolyn was frank.

He reached down, picked up a small stone and threw it into the water. "You know why I married her. I wanted the estate, and she came with it."

Carolyn looked over at him. "Are you sorry?"

"No. I knew the terms. We've managed to have it look respectable. She's not in good health, Carolyn. I suggested she stay here until she had seen a doctor, but she refused. Said if she was going to die, she wanted to die in her homeland."

"She was born here in Virginia, wasn't she?" said Carolyn.

Then he snickered. "She always believed she was related to the queen."

"Is she seriously ill?"

He nodded, then he changed the subject. "Are you happy? When Asa was missing during the war, I thought if he didn't return, maybe there was a chance for me."

Carolyn shook her head. "We had a lot of good times here when I took care of Mrs. Caldwell. You had your chance. I am very happy with my husband. You'll find someone if you find yourself a widower. You're like Andrew. The women always seemed to clamor for your attention."

James laughed. "I'm glad I came to talk to you, Miss Carolyn. You always set me straight." He rose, turned to leave and saw Asa walking in the direction of the pond. "Oh, oh," he said. "I believe Asa is coming to your rescue once again." He offered Carolyn his hand and helped her up.

Asa was there in a few strides. "Hello, James," he said.

"Hello, Asa. Your wife and I were talking over old times."

"I'm sure there were many to reminisce about." He took his place by Carolyn's side and offered his arm. "We should be getting back to the guests," Asa said to Carolyn.

James gave a slight bow and headed back to the crowd.

At the food table, Addie Lockwood was feeling a bit out of place as Alex was involved with a group of men who wanted his advice. He wasn't a lawyer anymore, but who could pass up free advice?

Claire Murphy came and stood next to her. "Are you from around here?" she asked Addie. "I'm Claire Murphy from Washington. I came with Mr. West and his sister."

"Adelaide Lockwood," she introduced herself. "Yes, I live on the other end of the county.

I don't know a lot of the people here. My husband is over there." She pointed. "He's the one in the tan suit." Addie hoped her face didn't show the expression of surprise at learning Harry's other guest was his sister.

"I'm not married," said Claire. "This is a lovely setting. I much prefer the country instead of the city."

Addie picked up a small cookie. "I worked in Washington during the war, and I was happy to come back home. Although I do sometimes miss all that the city has to offer."

"I work for Miss Ella as a clerk, but I'm taking classes at Katherine Gibbs to become a secretary."

Addie almost dropped her cookie. "I can't believe it. That's where I went to school."

Claire smiled at her. "For both us feeling a bit out of place, I think providence has brought us together." They found two chairs and sat to talk.

Elizabeth had been so busy being the perfect hostess she hadn't had time to sit with her friends. She saw Claire and Adelaide talking and was pleased as they both looked somewhat isolated. She looked at Claire. What was it about the young woman that nagged at her?

Elizabeth looked all around and was satisfied. There was a group around the music stand, a group of church women, men talking business, a politician making the rounds to discern who could do him the most good, and the upper crust gathered discussing the importance of boarding school not only to get ahead, but to find suitable mates.

Ella Fleming seemed to be right at home. She was as charismatic as her brother. Harry had taken an interest in Andrew's horses and asked about investing in a promising race horse. Harry West, the waiter at the Battletown Inn investing in a race horse?

Elizabeth Caldwell was standing by herself for a brief moment. Claire Murphy was also by herself as Alex had finished with his group and had taken Adelaide to meet someone. Adelaide apologized and Claire said she didn't mind sitting by herself. Then she spied Elizabeth and walked over to her.

"Do you remember me, Mrs. Caldwell?" she asked.

Elizabeth shook her head. "I'm sorry. I don't, although I feel I have met you before."

"Yes, that's when I was the novice, Sister Mary Claire at the orphanage."

Elizabeth gasped and grasped both of Claire's hands in hers. "Oh, my dear God!" she exclaimed in a soft voice. "If it hadn't been for you, I may never have found my baby."

"Do you need to sit down?" Claire asked as she caught a note of unsteadiness as Elizabeth stood there.

Elizabeth shook her head. "I'm alright. I need a minute to get over the shock."

"I recognized you the minute we came. You still have those clear blue eyes."

Elizabeth looked around and saw no one in earshot. In a confidential voice she said, "People here think Matthew's father is dead. They know Andrew adopted him. They don't know he was placed in an orphanage for the first months of his life."

"There's no need for them to know. Your private business is safe with me. How is Matthew?"

"He's a joy. He will be in second grade when school starts." Elizabeth saw a group of children playing near the barn. "He's in that group someplace. Be sure you meet him before you leave. I hope you didn't have to leave the order because you found my letter that Mother Superior was throwing in the wastebasket."

Claire smiled. "That was bold of me, wasn't it? No, I left because I didn't have the dedication required to be a nun. I left on good terms."

"I understand you work for Mrs. Fleming. Is that right?" said Elizabeth.

"I'm training to be a secretary. When I left the nunnery, I had enough money to rent a room for a few days. I am a firm believer in the Almighty, and He led me to Ella. Just as He's led me to you," Claire said. "I'm still not one to go to gatherings, but I am having an enjoyable time." Then she grinned. "I only came because I didn't want Ella to have to travel on the train by herself."

Elizabeth had dropped Claire's hands, but she reached for one again. "I want you to know that you are welcome to visit anytime."

At that point, Harry West came to where they stood. "Claire, would you like to go and listen to the music?"

Elizabeth dropped Claire's hand and looked at Harry. "We have been having a most interesting conversation, Harry. I'm glad you brought these ladies."

Harry smiled. "So am I." He offered his arm and escorted the prim Claire to the bandstand. Elizabeth smiled to herself as she watched them go. Harry West was a puzzle.

Carolyn made the rounds of visiting with people while Asa was talking business with other businessmen. It seemed Ella Fleming had their ear. Word got around that she was the owner of an investment firm in Washington. The stylish Ella Fleming was in her element. There was money to invest in Clarke County.

Ruth and Preston Bass had been with the group who made the rounds of the stables. While many of the women who were into horses weren't so much into style, Ruth Caldwell Bass was and always had been. She could be showy without appearing brassy. Today, she was in a green musketeer hat with a plume, and wore a green fitted jacket and skirt of imported fine virgin Merino wool. A white ruffled waist accented the outfit. She had once been the Belle of Red Gate. Although her time in England had mellowed her brash personality, Ruth remembered the time she was considered close to royalty at the Harvest Ball at Red Gate. Today she wanted to portray that role she had once played. If she couldn't be in a ball gown, she would garner the attention by her elegant attire. Ruth had changed, but old habits are difficult to break.

It was after three o'clock and time for the final dessert of strawberry shortcake and hand-cranked vanilla ice cream. Lavinia had the photographer taking pictures of the whole process.

The children gobbled theirs down, so they could have one more half hour of playful fun. The musicians had finished and came to have dessert along with everyone else before they packed up their instruments.

The first aid station had been used twice, once for a splinter and once for a skinned elbow. Guests were beginning to say their goodbyes, and Lavinia wanted one more photograph as the sun was moving into the western sky. The Blue Ridge looked very blue at this time of day.

Carolyn was going to find Annie and John Patrick while Catherine and Patrick were talking to the Hawthornes. Carolyn could see the children chasing one of the big playful farm dogs. She stopped in her tracks when she saw what was coming but was helpless to prevent it.

The dog ran from the children chasing him to where Lavinia was directing Jimmy to get a picture of the pond with the mountains behind it. There was a loud shriek and "AAAAAH!" The dog had run behind Lavinia's knees, and she went flying into the murky pond.

All heads turned toward the pond to witness the round Lavinia tumbling toward her christening. Patrick saw the upset and went racing past Carolyn who was on her way to the rescue.

Lavinia was crawling to the side of the pond when he reached her. She was drenched to the skin. Her hat, still pinned to her hair, sat askew on the side of her head, her face was mud splattered as were her clothes. And, Jimmy had time to turn his fancy new Kodak camera on its tripod to capture the scene. Snap!

Carolyn was sure she saw a satisfied smile on Jimmy's face when he removed the plate from the camera.

By that time Asa had come to aid Lavinia. Andrew was coming from the hop kiln carrying a blanket. "Bring her here," he called.

Lavinia was on her feet and sputtering, trying to recover from the shock. Once inside the makeshift first aid station, Patrick checked to be sure there was nothing injured except her dignity. Lavinia's ample form lay on the narrow cot, still wrapped in the blanket, gasping and breathing hard. Andrew brought her a glass of water.

She looked at him. Even through her gasps she wasn't at a loss for words. "That's a fine way to treat a guest. You should train your dogs!" Then she looked at all three and added, "Along with your children!"

Carolyn came to the door. "Do you need help?"

Patrick was swallowing a smile. "A dry blanket. I believe Mrs. Talley needs to rest a few minutes before she goes home."

Carolyn left to get a blanket and passed Jeremy on the way. "Patrick says she'll be fine. I'm sorry this happened."

Jeremy gave a quirky smile and shook his head. "Maybe she'll make the *Courier*."

Carolyn stifled a laugh. Jeremy Talley had a sense of humor.

It was after Lavinia's attraction that most of the guests had gone or were leaving before Carolyn got back to the lawn. Catherine had John Patrick and Annie waiting.

Harry West and his guests were some of the last to leave, but not before Claire Murphy was introduced to Matthew.

"Your mother says you're going to be a second grader," said Claire.

"I'm almost seven," replied a proud Matthew. "I can ride a horse. Why don't you come back and watch me?"

Claire gave a benevolent smile. "I would like that, but I live quite far away."

"Washington isn't that far away," chimed in Harry. "Perhaps that can be arranged."

Once they had gone, Elizabeth said, "I like Claire."

"From the looks of it, so does Harry," said Carolyn. "And, did I spy James Anderson escorting Ella Fleming to Harry's Maxwell?"

Catherine shook her head. "I don't believe you missed a thing all afternoon."

"I tried to best Lavinia," Carolyn replied.

"How is Lavinia?" asked Elizabeth.

"Blaming the dog and Andrew for not training it. Also, apparently we have been remiss in training our children," answered Carolyn."

"I wanted this day to be so perfect, and I think it was up to that point. I'll never live it down," moaned Elizabeth.

"Your party will be the talk of the whole county," Catherine agreed.

"Personally," said Carolyn, "I believe Lavinia was the star attraction. The sight of her climbing out of the pond will lift my day every time I picture it."

"That was a spectacular entry into the water," said Catherine. "I saw heads turn away to cover their smiles."

The two friends laughed aloud, but Elizabeth shook her head. "Poor Lavinia. I'm sure she was humiliated."

"Don't feel too sorry," Carolyn said. "You haven't yet heard how she'll twist the story around so it will be your fault."

The three women watched from the back lawn as Jimmy drove the car down the lane to the hop kiln. Jeremy opened the back door. Andrew and Asa assisted Lavinia into the back seat. Patrick closed the door of the first aid station and came to the back lawn.

They were sitting at a round table while behind them the children played marbles. Andrew and Asa came to sit with them.

Andrew kissed Elizabeth's cheek. "I believe your party was a hit." He lowered himself into a chair beside her.

"It was," said Asa. "Now, everyone will expect one every year."

"Do you think we can have the grand finale of pushing Lavinia into the pond? That was better than fireworks," commented Patrick.

They all laughed aloud.

Elizabeth groaned. "Aside from that, it was a success as everyone was talking to everyone before it was over. I saw old friendships renewed and new friendships formed. There was a feeling of community."

Catherine turned toward Patrick, "We need to be heading home to relieve Mary Lee."

"Wait a couple minutes," said Elizabeth. "There's one more thing." She went into the house and returned with a big box which she set in front of Catherine. "Go ahead and open it."

Catherine raised her eyebrows. But she opened the top and peeked inside "Oh my gosh!"

She stood up and lifted out a two layer cake surrounded by tiny pink roses and thirty candles on top.

"Happy birthday, Catherine. I know it is a day early. Carolyn and I wanted to surprise you."

"You certainly accomplished that." Catherine counted each of the candles to make sure there wasn't one extra.

"How did you remember?"

"Carolyn told me," said Elizabeth. "We couldn't let your milestone birthday pass."

"We need to sing Happy Birthday," Carolyn said. "Who wants to start it?"

The children gave up the marble game when they heard the word "cake".

"I will," said Matthew. "I know how to sing it."

It took three long wood matches before Andrew got the candles lit. Then he pointed to

Matthew, and they all joined in with the Happy Birthday song.

"Come on you three," Catherine said to the children. "I'll never blow them all out by myself." So together she and the three youngsters took a deep breath and blew. Then everyone clapped.

"That took one collective breath," said Patrick. "Is that fair?"

"It is if you want a piece of cake," Asa said. "I'll take a piece with a lot of frosting."

Ollie brought out cups, plates, forks, spoons, a pot of coffee, and glasses of milk for the children.

"Ollie, did you make this cake?" asked Carolyn.

"Yes, ma'am," she answered.

"I thank you. It's almost too pretty to eat," Catherine remarked.

Ollie gave a shy smile and disappeared into the house.

Andrew poured the coffee while Elizabeth cut and served the cake. They sat around the table recapping the events of the day. Harry West was the big surprise. They found he was not only the waiter, but the owner of the Battletown Inn. His monthly check went into investments. The frugal man who rented an upstairs apartment and drove an older model automobile was worth a bundle of money. His sister also had impressed them that a woman could run a successful business without the guidance of a man. In fact, they were going to look into investing their extra money.

All in all, it had been a good time, and they were tired. Elizabeth put what was left of the cake back in the box for Catherine to take home. They said goodbye with a promise to get together more often.

When Catherine and Patrick arrived home, John Patrick hurried up the steps before Catherine. Patrick pulled the car to the back of the house and took what was left of the cake into the kitchen.

"We're home," announced John Patrick in a loud voice. Catherine stepped into the foyer and Carrie Jo came running to meet her followed by Mary Lee holding Mary Margaret, who had her arms outstretched toward Catherine. Catherine took her from Mary Lee and kissed the child's cheek. "I missed my girls."

"We had a good afternoon," Mary Lee said. "There were no problems, and I didn't even have to ask any questions of Mattie. If you need me again, Miz' Catherine, you just let me know."

"Thank you Mary Lee. I'll do that," and she handed her an envelope of money.

Patrick came into the small group. "I have the car out back, Mary Lee. I'll take you home when you're ready."

"It's still light enough, I can walk," she said.

"You will not," was Catherine's adamant reply.

Mary Lee knew there was no room for argument. She smiled. "Yes, ma'am."

Still the cute little Mary Lee, she turned to Patrick. "Thank you, Doctor Burke. That will be right kind of you. I'm ready now."

They left through the kitchen. The three Burke children were back in the playroom. Catherine unpinned her hat, dropped it on the foyer table, and went into the living room where she sat in a soft chair.

What a wonderful and eventful day it had been. It was good to be home, although she would have to put the children to bed. Then she heard the kitchen door close and within a few seconds, Mattie was standing before her.

Catherine was surprised. "Mattie, I thought you were to rest."

"I done rested and it's time I got my babies changed into their night clothes."

Catherine smiled at her. "I won't say that isn't necessary, but I am worn out."

Mattie shook her head. "That's what them big doin's will do. I saw Mistah' Patrick leave with your helper, so you jus' sit there and I'll make you a nice cup of tea."

Catherine held up a halting hand. "Oh, that's not necessary."

"No, it ain't, but you look like you could use one."

Catherine chuckled. "I guess my age is showing."

Mattie just looked at her, offered an empathetic smile and left to brew the tea.

Catherine smiled to herself, satisfied with her life. It was good to be home, it was good to be turning thirty, and it was good that the garden party was over.

Other Books by Millie Curtis

Beyond the Red Gate

The Milliner

The Newcomer

Window of Hope

Of Course She Knew!

Never a Sure Thing

Roseville's Blooming Lilly

English Lessons

The Itchy Foot

Sisters of Mercy